A Better Looking Corpse

And Other Southern Short Stories

Best Wishes,

A Better Looking Corpse

And Other Southern Short Stories

Larry Larance

Windchimes Press

Manufactured in the United States of America

Library of Congress Control Number: 2007925635

ISBN 10: 0-9667665-3-9
ISBN 13: 978-0-9667665-3-0

Book design, cover design and production: Tabby House

Cover photo:
The Bradley County Courthouse, Warren, Arkansas, circa 1940, courtesy of Martha Blackwell Peters.

"No Forwarding Address" and "To Believe in Angels" first appeared in the 2006 anthology titled *Skidaway Musings.*

Windchimes Press
21 Rookery Road
Savannah, GA 31411

Dedication

Eugenia Ann Rhodes, our beloved Jean Jean

Contents

Introduction

Growing up in North Louisiana and Southeast Arkansas automatically exposed me to great tales. Members of my extended family were all inveterate storytellers. Jean Jean was my favorite. My maternal grandmother's real name was Eugenia Ann Rhodes. All the grandchildren had trouble pronouncing her name, and our attempts rearranged Eugenia into Jean Jean.

Jean Jean did not commit her stories to writing. She had no formal education and her handwriting was of an elementary variety. When she repeated a tale for the umpteenth time—as I had encouraged her to do—I would eventually know it by heart. A skilled seamstress, Jean Jean made beautiful quilts by piecing together scraps of cloth long since abandoned for original uses, including those from flour sacks of floral design. She could also perform magic with crochet needles. Her doilies are now framed as treasured pieces of family art. In the kitchen she prepared the most delicious Southern lunches any boy could imagine. I have tried unsuccessfully to reproduce her fried, hot-water bread, clearly the best tasting morsel in the immediate western world.

My grandmother was also the only person I ever knew to use snuff, a powdered form of tobacco prepared for sniffing. Her supply came in a distinctive brown bottle labeled Levi Garrett & Sons. She used the Sweet Mild brand and seemed always to have a pinch of it tucked under her lower lip. I didn't care for the scent of snuff, a sour musty odor that trailed her throughout the house. As a result, a handy spittoon was required.

Jean Jean was a homemaker and a farmer, tending children as well as a large garden. She also had a job, working from her home.

The front room of the five-room unpainted house outside the village of Hico, Louisiana, was set up as the switchboard for the community telephone system. My grandmother was the switchboard operator, a role female comedians love to use for skits. She took incoming calls and rerouted them to the intended parties, listening in on conversations if she wanted to. Grandmother Jean Jean had a few humorous skits of her own as a result.

She also had a wonderful memory for family tales and I took advantage of every opportunity to ask questions and persuade her to tell one of her stories. The best part was that most of them were self-deprecating and she found them funny. While trying to stay composed as she related an event, the process resulted in her breaking into spasms of laughter. This was always an uncontrolled, sidesplitting laughter that brought tears to her eyes. The harder she tried to suppress the giggles, the more intense they became. The emotional release was contagious and we had no choice but to join in. Almost all of her stories had an object lesson attached, establishing over time a set of values not lost on her grandchildren.

My grandfather and namesake, Charles Elbert Rhodes, died in 1918 at age forty-five, twenty years before I made my debut. He married my grandmother Jean Jean—whose maiden name was Hanks—on November 21, 1902, at home in Hico. She was seventeen when they married and had her first child at nineteen. She claimed to be a descendant of Nancy Hanks, the mother of President Abraham Lincoln. We were never able to authenticate such heritage.

Jean Jean was born in Blue Mountain, Alabama, on June 3, 1885. The Hanks family, like most in the region, was involved in subsistence agriculture. There were a handful of large plantations in the area, but most farmers worked small pieces of land, raising grains, vegetables, and tending a few livestock to feed their families. The Civil War broke up most of the plantations.

Some of my grandmother's most interesting memories had to do with how she ended up in Louisiana. All this happened at about the same time Orville and Wilber Wright were conducting flight experiments in Kitty Hawk, North Carolina. As a very young child—perhaps five or six years old—she traveled with her parents and other family members in covered wagons across Alabama to Northern Louisiana. There were only 144 miles of paved roads in the United States in 1900, confined mostly to city streets, and autos were fragile luxury items. In rural America most travel was by foot, carriage or wagon.

Families that had crossed the Mississippi earlier sent messages back to Blue Mountain with stories about cheap land in Louisiana, rich soil and good crops. The Hanks family decided to follow, eventually crossing the Big River on a barge. Jean Jean remembered at least two wagons, pulled by mules and oxen. The men drove the wagons, walking alongside the teams while the children walked behind. A single cow—called a milch cow—was tied to the last wagon and had to be milked every morning. They slept inside the wagons under the shelter of a watertight canvas bonnet. When the weather permitted, they slept under the wagons or under the stars.

The children had important jobs to do: feeding the animals, gathering firewood and bringing in fresh water from nearby streams. Jean Jean remembered two dolls made of cornhusks as her primary travel companions.

During a part of the journey they followed a trail developed in the 1800s known as the Natchez Trace. They traveled down the eastern side of the Mississippi River on a long section of the trail called the Devil's Backbone. The party eventually camped for a time on the bank of the river while building a barge and waiting for the low water season. The few bridges available in 1900 were railroad crossings, located many miles north in the Upper Mississippi Valley. For part of the trip they were accompanied by a small band of Indians—thought to be Choctaw—looking for more fertile land and hunting grounds. The Hanks were following recommendations of earlier pioneers in search of unoccupied land and farming opportunities in the West.

Southern writers and their short stories have always fascinated me. The South—especially of the 1940s and '50s—provided the perfect setting for the best tales with the most interesting characters, very real people experiencing all the triumphs and losses of life. People from the region grew up in a world of deeply ingrained tradition. It was always important to know and understand your parents, to spend as much time as possible with grandparents, following closely your lineage. Southerners develop self-knowledge and self-respect from this heritage. The stories of ancestors handed down from generation to generation provide a foundation for personal beliefs and values, one of the region's richest cultural traditions.

Common themes include a sense of belonging, closeness to the soil, strong family relationships, and an assortment of eccentric characters, all displayed through a rich tapestry of language. There is something of a love affair with words, exploring their meaning and finding unusual ways to use them. In the Deep South, roadways occasionally give in to kudzu vines, and live oak trees drip with Spanish moss. This is a land shrouded in mystery and romance, the perfect ingredients for memorable tales. I find the legends of the South just as intriguing and intricate as its myths.

Those of us from Dixieland don't talk rapid fire, not because we are less well educated or can't think quickly, rather because conversation is actually important to us. We like to listen for the music and taste the words. While working in the larger cities of the Northeast, I observed that conversation often took on the characteristics of a contest, a forced dash to an imaginary finish. A genuine effort to hear and understand another person was deemed a sign of weakness. The first of the participants to actually take a full breath would be declared "the listener."

It is instructional and entertaining to read and reread the works of Eudora Welty, Alice Walker, Peter Taylor, James Dickey, Charles Portis and Willie Morris. I first began thoughts of writing my own stories after reading *North Toward Home* by the Mississippi man of letters, Willie Morris:

> "I knew that one's life, one's spanning of years and places, could never be of a piece, but rather were like scattered fragments of old glass."
>
> —Willie Morris
> *North Toward Home*

It's hard to think of another part of the country where the writing craft is pursued with such passion. It's a great treat to curl up on a weekend afternoon with a cup of hot coffee and a new novel written by a writer from the South. These short stories represent a continuing apprenticeship on my part and a continuing attempt to become one.

—Larry Larance

A Kinder Cut

Union Grove, Arkansas
Population: 3,433

"Good Lord in heaven, Mrs. Threlkeld," said James Lewis Ashcraft, stepping from behind his barber chair for a closer look. "What'n the name of Jesus happened to Pookie?"

Mrs. Sarah Jean Threlkeld was pushing her grandson through the door of Ashcraft's Barber Shop on South Main Street, struggling with the seven-year-old's resistance to a much-needed trim. Russell Adair Threlkeld, known by all in the Union Grove community as Pookie, had Band-Aids on his forehead, each cheek and on both arms from the elbows to the wrists. He was not fazed by the attention, continuing to give his grandmother difficulty.

"Don't worry none," she sighed. "Pookie ain't hurt as bad as it looks."

"Did he fall in a briar patch?" asked James Lewis.

"Naw, but it's a right long story."

"Jest go ahead on, Mrs. Threlkeld. We got all day!"

"It started last Sunday morning at the Brotherhood Baptist Church. . . ." Mrs. Threlkeld struggled to guide the boy into a chair beside her. "Pookie saw the Reverend Watson baptize old Mrs. Carmichael, you know, the widow of Colvin Carmichael, who used to run the feed store out on the highway toward Jackson."

"I knew him," said James Lewis. "He used to come in for a trim."

"Old Mr. Carmichael died about a month ago of a heart attack. I think it was his heart . . . might'a been a stroke. Come to think of it, I don't believe it was his heart. Some say it was a stroke, but I ain't for sure what he died of."

She barely paused for a breath before adding, "All I know for certain is that Colvin is graveyard dead. He was funeralized at Frazer's Mortuary a few days later and they buried him at a cemetery near Possum Valley. I believe he moved here from Possum Valley about ten year ago. Anyway, I guess old Mrs. Carmichael thought it was time for her to get right with the Lord."

"What's all that got to do with Pookie?" asked James Lewis, impatience in his voice.

"Well, yesterday evening," she said with a frown, "Pookie tried to baptize our next door neighbor's cat!"

Wallace Dickson, who owned the Texaco Station at the corner of Main and Elm, was halfway out of the barber chair when Mrs. Threlkeld explained Pookie's dilemma, having just completed his regular Thursday shave and cut. Wallace was now doubled over holding his stomach. Two elderly regulars—Joe Willy Thornton and Billy Ray Williams—sat in metal chairs against the opposite wall. They couldn't look at each other, trying to suppress an explosion of laughter. They were not successful, slapping their knees and howling at the imagery.

This is why most of the citizens of Union Grove ventured in and out of Ashcraft's barber shop Tuesday through Saturday mornings. Since the shop was open on Saturday, James Lewis followed his uncle's tradition of closing on Mondays. Ashcraft's Barber Shop was the central meeting place for news about the issues of the day, discussions and debates on a wide range of regional topics, free coffee from the ever-steaming pot at the back, and entertainment such as that provided by the arrival of Pookie and his grandmother. It was, of course, also the place for Union Grove citizens to take care of certain grooming requirements. For the latest in hometown news or gossip, it was important to stop by Ashcraft's Barber Shop for coffee once or twice a week.

Union Grove tottered on the Arkansas side of the Delta just forty miles west of the Mississippi River. Cotton and soybean farmers worked the rich black soil, raised a little cattle, tended lush gardens, and made do with unpredictable grain prices. Every family had a pickup truck, a vegetable garden, several hound dogs, and a small fenced-in chicken yard.

James Lewis took a child's booster seat from the cabinet behind him, carefully placing it across the arms of his barber chair. He then removed two pieces of candy from a box on the counter. He waved lollypops at young Pookie. One was bright red, the other forest green.

"Come set yourself up in this chair, good buddy," he said with a smile, "and you can have both these when we finish your cut."

The bribe worked to perfection. Pookie shook loose from his grandmother and climbed up in the seat. He grinned in a mischievous way at those sitting across from him, a clear signal to the men folk present that he had been in control of the situation from the start.

James Lewis inherited the town's only barbershop in 1940 when his favorite uncle died unexpectedly. Uncle Elwood Ashcraft had smoked three packs of Camels a day since age fourteen. This led to the premonition that he would not be around much longer to cut hair and referee the debates in his shop. That's why he had urged his nephew to attend the Dixie Barber College in Jackson, Mississippi, shortly after graduation from high school. He even loaned James Lewis funds for the studies and helped him apply for his state barber's license. Elwood had promised him the second chair in the shop and suggested one day he could own a piece of the business. All that had happened much sooner than James Lewis expected. His uncle Elwood, a widower with no children of his own, left the shop to James Lewis in his will.

Ashcraft's reputation as the lively place on Main Street was conditioned in large part by the coffee. James Lewis ordered his coffee from a specialty house in New Orleans, a commercial brand sold primarily to restaurants. It was a dark roast variety with a tasteful hint of chicory. The aroma drifted up and down Main Street and served as a magnet for the usual morning gang.

Joe Willie Thornton and Billy Ray Williams arrived at the same time each weekday the shop was open. The pair appeared to have an abundance of spare time. Both retired in the same year and were never short on opinions about every topic of conversation. They were opposites in every way. Any issue of discussion was an open invitation to disagreement for them.

Joe Willie was outgoing, cheerful, always smiling and pleasant to all who entered the shop. He was short and stocky, slightly overweight and possessed a lively gift of gab. His hair was still dark, though there was not much of it. He had been retired for ten years, selling his corner grocery store to a man from the nearby town of Dumas. He turned over the keys and merchandise and never looked back. In fact, he had not been back to Thornton's Market but twice since. He and Billy Ray had become constant companions in retirement, as unlikely a pair as walked the earth.

At seventy-six, Billy Ray shuffled when he walked, dragging his left foot slightly. He seemed at times uncertain of his balance, moving with the same caution some folks use when they have had too much sour mash. Billy Ray constantly complained about the weather, teenagers, public officials, the state government and local preachers. The regulars at Ashcraft's weren't bothered by his bellyaching, simply finding him a source of amusement. For others, Billy Ray left a lasting impression that he was functioning with a combination of sore feet and hemorrhoids.

Marvin Reep came in the shop, removing his jacket and St. Louis Cardinals ball cap at the door. Marvin worked as janitor and all round handy man at the Union Grove Health Clinic. He wore blue denim overalls and a faded flannel shirt. The morning regulars at the barbershop assumed Marvin's outfit, or several exactly alike represented the total of his wardrobe. No one could every remember seeing Marvin Reep in anything other than overalls and a flannel shirt, even in the middle of summer.

The first chair was empty so Marvin climbed up to take his place, glancing over his shoulder at James Lewis as if to say, "Let's get on with it."

James Lewis moved behind the chair and shook out the shiny nylon cape he tucked under every client's chin, fastening it with a clip behind his neck. As usual, Marvin had gone too long without a haircut. His wife Claudine had, in the interim, been trimming Marvin's hair over the ears and at his neck, stretching out the time he would have to spend another fifty cents for a real professional cut. It was obvious to all present that Claudine's talent at the barbering business was severely limited.

"Been awhile since you been in," said James Lewis, lifting his head and raising his eyebrows at the men seated across the room. "Looks like you need some work on the sides and top."

"Just get'r done," grunted Marvin. "I ain't got a lot of time this morning."

"What is it?" cackled Billy Ray from the end chair, already working on a third cup of coffee. "You got a job interview with the mayor this morning at the courthouse?"

"Billy Ray, you ain't all that funny," responded Marvin, staring straight ahead, trying to keep a still head for his barber.

"Just leave Marvin alone, Billy Ray," said Joe Willie. "Can't you tell when a man is concentratin' and has lots of important stuff on his mind?"

"Like what stuff?"

"Well, he's probably worried about whether or not we should let Red China in the Eunited Nations. Might be he needs to finish a letter to Truman about the national debt."

Marvin glared at the both of them without saying anything. James Lewis tended to his haircutting and smiled to himself at the thought of Marvin Reep advising the president. He felt confident the morning would move along at its usual pace.

Fred Doggett stepped in off Main Street, his hat pulled low over his eyes and both hands pushed down in his pockets. He grunted a morning greeting to no one in particular and slumped into a chair across from barber chair one.

"Oh no!" said James Lewis. "Don't tell me, Fred! Did Sandra

Jean run you out of the house again this morning?"

Fred looked down the row of chairs against the wall, making certain he knew exactly who was present and who would be interested in his answer. The regulars were already aware of his ongoing troubles with a headstrong wife.

"It was just the usual," he said. "This time she wants me to go with her to Yazoo City next weekend for her brother's birthday party."

"Why don't you just go?" chimed in Billy Ray and Joe Willie in unison.

"I can't stand her brother, or his wife, and especially their three snotty-nosed kids. They are all maniacs!"

"Well," said Billy Ray, with a sigh, a huge grin forming at the corners of his mouth, "I hear tell that her brother speaks very highly of you!"

"You don't even know her brother, Billy Ray. And besides, you're about as funny as a root canal. Why don't you just keep them silly remarks to yourself."

"We all need to just give Fred some breathing room," offered Joe Willie. "Can't you see the man's experiencing some distress?"

It was a typical assortment of clients for the day. A steady stream of Union Grove patrons came and went. While several actually needed haircuts, most folks just stopped by for the coffee and social interplay.

Dr. Malcolm B. Carter, the oldest practicing doctor in Claiborne County, showed up for his regular Thursday morning shave and shampoo. At seventy-four, he was in better shape than most men in Union Grove half his age. Doc Carter's wife Sybil died eight years ago of cancer and he had been eyeing the young nurses and staffers at the Union Grove Clinic. His amorous behavior had been the source of several entertaining tales at the barbershop.

The talk of the town for the past month was Dr. Carter's recent marriage to his receptionist, a thirty-eight-year-old blond named Maggie Jean Wentworth. Maggie Jean was not blessed with an inquiring mind. While she was no beauty in the classic sense, she was well-endowed in several physical aspects. So well, in fact, that the barbershop talk included serious concern for Doc Carter's health; that is, his potential stamina. It was difficult to tell if the concern was genuine or tongue-in-cheek.

"Good morning, Doc," chimed Billy Ray and Joe Willie. "How's that new bride of yours doing?"

"She's doing just fine, fellers," said Doc Carter, removing his eyeglasses and handing them to James Lewis as he made his way into the barber chair. "Thank you for asking."

"I think it's just wonderful of you to rescue that girl," said Joe Willie. "I was wondering how it is to have a new wife so much younger than yourself."

James Lewis frowned at Joe Willie from behind the barber chair, signaling the need for a change of subject. Joe Willie didn't see the signal or simply ignored it.

"Doc, how in the world do you keep up with that Maggie gal?" asked Billy Ray.

"You should think about getting married again yourself," offered Doc Carter. " It's just a wonderful thing to have new female companionship."

"Once was enough for me," said Joe Willie, a serious frown appearing at just the thought of another wife. "I believe freedom to come and go as you please is an even more wonderful thing."

Doc sighed. "Every evening when I come home from the clinic Maggie Jean is waiting to shower me with kisses."

"I got me a big bluetick hound dog by the name of Rascal," said Joe Willie, "and he does that same thing for me when I come home. In fact, on the weekends he even licks my white wall tires."

"That's about enough of that," interjected James Lewis, but to no avail.

"I can even feed ol' Rascal for about two bits a day. . . . How much does that Maggie gal cost you?"

Assuming a role not unfamiliar to the two protagonists, James Lewis held his left hand up to Joe Willie, as if halting traffic, and pointed his right index finger directly at Billy Ray.

"That's entirely enough on that subject, fellows!" he said with understood authority. "Doc Carter and I need to discuss something far more important."

"What's that?" asked the doctor, turning his head to look at James Lewis, as if to question his seriousness.

"The important question we need to be asking this morning is: Can the Union Grove Bulldogs beat the Perryville Ravens next Friday night?"

"The new coach is our biggest problem," offered the doctor.

"Them boys knew the Slot-T formation backwards and forwards," said Billy Ray.

"When that new coach changed to the single wing they got all confused, especially that junior quarterback Travis Henry."

Joe Willie chimed in: "Henry was a darn good quarterback before the new coach—ain't his name Scobey or something?—changed things all around. A couple more losses in a row and some of the good old boys around here might be taking Coach Scobey out behind the ice house for a discussion."

"You better not mess with the new coach because he is about the smartest man in Harmony Grove," said the doctor. "If you don't believe it, jest ask him."

There was a nodding agreement from all assembled.

"It don't take a second for the coach to let you know what he thinks on any subject," said James Lewis. "He's got a answer to jest about everything!"

The former coach had produced a winning season three out of the last four years. The citizens of Union Grove had gotten used to the bragging rights. He was lured away to a larger job at a higher division school in Pine Bluff, leaving Union Grove to start over.

Coach David Scobey tried to impress Union Grove folks with his advanced college degree and plans for working on a doctorate. The barbershop crowd thought the coach was still damp behind the ears, or so the conversations suggested each Saturday morning during the postgame critiques.

Coach Scobey had played football for Arkansas State in the town of Jonesboro, and earned a master's in education at the University of Arkansas. He had been an assistant coach at a high school in Hamburg for only two years before taking the head coach position at Union Grove. The regulars at Ashcraft's Barber Shop considered the new coach long on talk and short on results. The local football fans were not often impressed with people who held themselves in high regard. Coach Scobey fit nicely into that category.

"Coach Scobey strikes me as all hat and not much cowboy," said Billy Ray.

"What'd you think it would take to have him change back to the Slot-T?" asked Joe Willie.

"About two more losses," said the doc.

The entire assembly at the barbershop sat silent for a few minutes, thinking about what the doctor said and trying to imagine the citywide relief that would accompany the change back to an offensive alignment familiar to both the players and local fans.

The door opened and a young blond stepped inside. The conversation came to an immediate halt as James Lewis and his patrons ogled.

"Mr. McReynolds sent me down to ask if y'all wanted to git your lunch orders in now before the noon crowd?"

James Lewis and several of his regulars ordered lunch each weekday from Mac's Confectionery at the corner of Main and Bradley. They seemed frozen in place at the sight of this lovely young woman, a new employee they had not seen before. Mac's wife Adeline usually came down to take orders. And while Adeline was not an unattractive woman, this young lady taking her place took them by surprise.

"I don't believe we've met," said James Lewis, breaking a silence that seemed much longer than it actually was.

"I'm sorry," she said. "I am Barbara Lynn McReynolds. Mr. Mac is my uncle and I am working here for the summer."

"That's great," said Doc Carter. "How long will you be in Union Grove?"

"Uncle Mac said I could work until the next semester starts at

Louisiana Tech."

"Well, welcome to Union Grove," said James Lewis. "It's very nice to have a new face at Mac's place."

Joe Willie and Billy Ray sat transfixed with their mouths open. Doc Carter glanced over his shoulder at James Lewis, his eyes wide and a pencil-thin grin forming at the corners of his mouth. Barbara Lynn was so stunningly beautiful that she took their collective breaths.

Turns out that Barbara Lynn was the daughter of Mr. Mac's younger brother Roger who ran an auto repair business in El Dorado, Arkansas. At twenty, she would be starting her junior year at Tech, majoring in elementary education. She tired of the usual summer jobs in department stores and had endured a bad experience the past summer as an intern in the personnel department of a large financial services company in El Dorado. A couple of months at the corner café with her uncle would provide some much-needed spending money and a break from larger city life.

Doc Carter retrieved his glasses, paid for services rendered, and tipped his hat to the young lady as he headed out the door. James Lewis ordered his usual: chicken salad sandwich, an apple, bag of Fritos and large Royal Crown cola. Joe Willie and Billy Ray couldn't think of anything but BLT sandwiches and stammered to order those. Barbara Lynn wrote notes on a pad and thanked them as she closed the door behind her.

"Whoa, Nellie!" said Billy Ray. "She's right near the prettiest girl I have ever seen in my en-tire life!"

Joe Willie couldn't resist: "Her parents should of won the Nobel Prize for architecture."

"She is really something," suggested James Lewis, "and the lunchtime business at Mac's is going to pick up when the word gets around among all the hairy-legged boys 'round here."

"She ought'a be a movie star or a model," said Billy Ray. "They ain't another female in this county that comes anywhere close to her looks."

"If I was only twenty years younger," sighed Joe Willie. "I'd be sporting that gal."

"In your case it would take fifty years younger," laughed Billy Ray. "If you was to have a romantic half hour with that gal followed by a cold glass of ice water, it would kill you dead as hell!"

"Fellas, ya'll are having impure thoughts," said James Lewis. "I want you both to just change the subject. She's gonna be back here directly with our lunches."

She did return with their food, collected the pay, and backed out the door, leaving them with a Southern girl smile that could bring on mild diabetes.

Billy Ray and Joe Willie left shortly after lunch, both indicating they had other chores for the afternoon. Billy Ray had to change a tire on his ancient pickup truck, and Joe Willie had to stop by Wilson's Feed & Seed to pick up some fungicide for his tomato plants. He said he might also stop by the Farmers' Market to see if he could pick up a mess of collard greens for supper. They all agreed that fresh collards sounded like a good idea.

Before James Lewis could sweep up clippings and do his usual mid-afternoon house cleaning, in came the mayor.

"Afternoon to you, Mr. James Lewis Ashcraft," he said in a loud voice as if addressing a crowd of voters.

"I was expecting you, Mister Mayor," he grinned. "About time for that weekly shave and cut."

Mayor Franklin P. Withers was in his second and, as he reminded all, last term of office. A man of ample girth, the mayor was almost a caricature of himself: loud, outspoken, a glad-hander, backslapper and "hail-fellow-well-met." He was never seen in public without a coat and tie, carefully switching from brown to blue. It appeared to the citizens of Union Grove that the mayor owned only two ties; that is, he seemed always to wear one or the other. With the brown suit he wore the blue tie. With the blue suit, the brown tie.

Today was different. The mayor was disheveled. His navy blue suit was wrinkled, his white shirt unbuttoned at the collar and his brown tie hanging loose at his chest.

"What's wrong Mister Mayor?" he asked. "You having a bad day?"

"You wouldn't believe it," he exclaimed, "I'd turn this job over to you in a minute. Today I might even pay you to take it."

"Couldn't be that bad?"

The mayor took off his coat and tie, hung them on the rack and climbed in the barber chair.

"First thing this morning I get a call from old Mrs. Baggett. . . . I think her name is Rachel. Anyway, she is complaining again about a drainage ditch next to her property."

"What's the problem?"

"She is screeching at me about the ditch being stopped up and why don't I do something about it. I have called Joe Don Adkins at the water works twice about it, and he tells me they have been out there and can't find no problem."

"Some say old Mrs. Baggett ain't right in the head."

"Bless her heart," sighed the mayor, "I believe the woman is several bricks short of a full load."

James Lewis leaned the mayor's head back and began lathering his chin with shaving soap. The mayor squirmed to free his mouth, a signal that he was not through talking. "The old bat can't remember for an hour that she just called me, and turns right around and calls again with the same stuff. She's about to drive me to a hissy fit!"

"Somebody should call Mrs. Baggett's daughter about her condition, I think she lives in Monticello."

The mayor was also upset about a new problem with the upcoming Union Grove Soybean Festival. Adrian Adair, manager of the Franklin Five & Dime on Main Street had agreed to be chairman of the annual festival, and had begun recruiting citizens to head up the dozens of committees required for the four-day event.

With a mixture of resignation and disgust in his voice, he said, "Just yesterday Adrian announced that he was being transferred to Little Rock to manage a larger store in the Franklin group, and that he would be moving right away."

The mayor was in a predicament. He had no replacement at this eleventh hour, and no one was stepping up to fill the post. He had pleaded with Adrian to at least continue to manage the several committees long distance, but it was of no use.

"I been talking to lots of folks, calling in some chits, trying everything I could think of to find a new Soybean chairman. I ain't having no luck. How 'bout you, James Lewis?"

"Thanks, but no thanks. I gotta run this barbershop."

"As if that wasn't enough, about a half hour after them two calls from that screeching Rachel Baggett, Buddy Sullivan came by to tell me the deputy had wrecked our other patrol car!"

"You gotta be kidding."

"Nope. Seems old Marvin couldn't make the turn at West Pine Street, just across from the plywood mill. He ran into a big oak tree and the front end of that squad car is a mess. At least he didn't hit nobody."

"Didn't that same deputy tear up your other police car a few weeks ago?"

"Yep, just got it back from the garage last Tuesday. The Union Grove police force is made up of morons. I would get better people for the job, but we don't pay'm nothing. So, we gets what we pays for."

They both watched a mother pass the shop window pushing a baby carriage.

"Guess we're lucky to have no crime to speak of," added the mayor, "that is, if we don't count Booger Winsloe. He always seems to have a steady supply of Jack Daniels even though this is a dry county. We can't figure out where he gets the stuff."

This time James Lewis lathered the mayor's upper lip and chin. He set about sharpening his straight razor on a leather strap hanging from behind the chair. He then pinched the mayor's nose with the thumb and forefinger of his left hand and began shaving with the razor in his right. He worked quickly and efficiently, demonstrating a skill born of much practice.

When James Lewis began his haircut, the mayor again launched into the troubles of the morning at city hall. His secretary, Betty Lynn

Bradbury, announced that she is pregnant.

"The gal is pregnant again," exclaimed the mayor. " I think there's entirely too much unnecessary diddling going on in this county!"

James Lewis laughed out loud: "You wouldn't be saying that if you was twenty years younger!"

The mayor sighed and reviewed his problems of the moment. "I can't find a new chairman for the Soybean Festival. Them calls from Ms. Baggett jest never cease. The second of my city police patrol cars went back to collision repair and my secretary is pregnant for the fourth time."

"You might want to consider taking a brief vacation," offered the barber, and the mayor did not reply.

James Lewis finished the cut, removed the nylon cover, dusted the mayor off with a whiskbroom and collected his fee.

Mayor Withers appeared to have caught a second wind. He took a deep breath, fastened his tie back in place and slung his suit coat over his shoulder. He stopped at the door and looked back.

"What do you think? . . . Would it be against the law if I went over to Rachel Baggett's house right now and choked her to death?"

"Yes, sir, Mister Mayor, I believe that would be against both state and federal law."

"Thanks, James Lewis. I know I can always count on you for sound legal and political advice."

The door closed to Main Street and for the first time since early that morning, Ashcraft's Barber Shop was quiet. The coffeepot was almost empty. James Lewis poured himself the last cup, sat in the front chair and looked out the window. Foot traffic had almost disappeared from the street. Most of the shoppers were finished for the day. It was going to be a sleepy autumn evening in Union Grove.

It had been another good day at Ashcraft's Barber Shop. He thought, *I made a few bucks, had lots of laughs, met a beautiful young lady new to the café, and put up with the usual crowd of crackpots that assemble here almost every day.*

Sometimes these folks almost drive me nuts, he thought, *but I love 'em to death and they are really like family. Life was actually pretty darn good right there in Union Grove.*

James Lewis decided to close the shop early. He could be out to Roy Lander's pond in twenty minutes. He had a new Lucky 13 artificial bait to try out and the large mouth bass ought to be hitting around dusk.

The Fortune

Millwood, Louisiana
Population: 4,476

Tiny legs moved in a rhythmic pattern, inching along the stem of a fallen twig and back to the soggy earth below. A wet leaf interrupted the journey, resulting in a momentary detour. Back on course, one thin leg at a time onto and around the obstacle until they blended into uniform progress. It moved across the soft underfooting and around a large acorn, down the remaining ribs of another leaf and back to the dark soil.

Rain does not lighten the burden of an ant. The smallest drop is an inconvenience. A late afternoon shower in the spring brings cobwebs to the ground and the earth is always sticky afterwards. Puddles that form result in many extra inches to travel when time is important and the destination near. The trek is made more difficult with the fading evening light. The lives of ants are conditioned by a tribal environment, dependent on strict rules and carefully orchestrated internal working units. Assignments must be taken seriously and expectations are that each will be completed on schedule and in harmony with the several interdependent alliances.

The earth shook and a woman's sandal suddenly closed the ant's path. No need for alarm. This happens often and life's smallest creatures are experienced in such accommodations. This obstruction, not unlike many, must be crossed if the journey is to continue. The objective is to reach safety by nightfall.

The ant moves on, up the heel and halfway down the sole, around the strap and across the naked ankle. The skin is damp and it is hard to maintain footing. A swift rush of air comes out of the evening sky and life ends with the silent pressure of a thumb.

Night birds cry somewhere in the distance. The sound that fills the air is not of pain. It is more a cry of hopelessness. Other creatures come out of hiding. They stand and watch. They try to weep. If they do, it is only for an instant and their tears run quickly to join the raindrops. The anguish is but for a moment and we do not know if they mourned the passing.

That thumb is attached to a slender hand with unkempt nails. It belongs to a young woman of thirty-four years, whose face and figure leave no lasting impression. Her clothes are assembled around her body in a disheveled fashion and her hands smell of cheap perfume.

Eddie Mae Colvin is not an attractive woman. She is unaware that her tastes in fashion compound the problem. She lives in the narrow reality of her own design. That is not unusual in the small southern towns of the late 1950s. Millwood, in the Louisiana hill country, is located east of Shreveport and just south of the Arkansas line. This is oil well territory, where many of the landowners happened into extra income through leases to oil companies in search of new natural resources. However, the majority of work is in the timber industry, in small cattle operations, or in trying to farm in the red clay of Stillwell Parish.

The Colvin family had been merchants in the region since the 1860s when Eddie Mae's great grandparents, Ephraim and Ethel Grace, traveled west from the Carolinas in a covered wagon. They joined other travelers trying desperately to escape fighting by the Blue and Gray along the eastern seaboard. Ephraim brought his family to North Louisiana and settled in a village called Millwood. He bought a bit of acreage and built a small frame house at the edge of the community.

Shortly afterwards he opened a general mercantile store on the muddy Main Street. The store remained in the family through three generations, with Eddie Mae's father the last of the Colvin boys with any interest in keeping the store open. Her parents—Percy and Cornelia—lived in the old Colvin family home, remodeled several times over the years with add-ons by each succeeding generation. Over time the store was successful enough to expand, even offering a line of inexpensive furniture during the most prosperous years. Percy was now growing tired and a CLOSED sign appeared more often in the store window. Patronage dwindled.

Eddie Mae had been a late and unexpected arrival for Percy and Cornelia. After trying for more than a decade, they resigned themselves to the reality of a barren union. Cornelia was in her mid-forties when Eddie Mae was born. It was a difficult pregnancy from which she never fully recovered. The couple was pleased to welcome the addition to the family, but strangely detached from emotional involvement in the care of a newborn.

Eddie Mae's mother and father did not display public affection for her, or for each other.

They found dealing with an infant awkward and disruptive to the comfortable and uneventful routine of their lives. Cornelia died of cancer when Eddie Mae was eleven years old, and Percy accepted the responsibility of raising their daughter through adolescence, a task he was ill-equipped to handle. As the years passed, Eddie Mae found herself parenting a parent, a role she accepted willingly and with which she was entirely comfortable. Taking care of the chores at home and looking after her father gave Eddie Mae a sense of importance, something she never experienced in school. She found the academic work difficult and was not interested in studies. Her grades at Millwood High School were barely passing and she managed to always sit in the back of the class, hoping not to be called on or recognized for any reason. To that end Eddie Mae was successful; that is, she was generally ignored by her classmates and merely acknowledged or tolerated by her teachers. An uneventful high school graduation came and went. Eddie Mae had no college ambitions.

Her role as companion and housekeeper for her aging father

continued, but she grew anxious about what would happen when her father closed the store. His health was also fading and Eddie Mae tried not to think about what she would do when Percy died, the prospect was simply too stressful. Her weekly activities took on a dreadful sameness. She prepared breakfast oatmeal for her father, read the Style Section of the *Shreveport Times*, cleaned, dusted, did laundry and worked in the garden or her flowerbeds as appropriate to the schedule and season.

She did have a few older women acquaintances from the ladies' auxiliary at the Freewill Baptist Church and she talked over the fence with the neighbor lady next door, Ida Jeanette Upchurch. Ida made trips to the back of her garage several times a day. That's where she kept her "medicine." Ida Jeanette maintained a generous supply of a cure-all elixir called Hadacol.

Louisiana State Senator Dudley LeBlanc traveled to small towns all over East Texas, Arkansas, Louisiana, and Mississippi with a large supply of his medicine in a white-paneled truck, blasting a sales pitch about the virtues of Hadacol from a booming sound system. His caravan included a Hadacol country music band, entertaining the locals from a flat-bed truck. Sales were brisk.

Ida Jeanette claimed to suffer from rheumatism and the clear liquid was her medicine of choice. The neighborhood knew she ordered it in the quart bottle size and kept a supply hidden in the garage. She thought husband Lewis knew only about the small four-ounce container she took along to the beauty parlor, to quilting bees and to her Wednesday night prayer meetings. Her neighbors were skeptics, later justified in their concerns as the Food and Drug Administration's findings revealed what the Hadacol label did not: that it was a 140 proof alcohol, primarily an Ever Clear vodka with a dash of bitters. The taste was medicinal but not so bad as to discourage Ida Janette from regular doses.

Lewis Upchurch operated his own pulpwood business and worked seven days a week, leaving Ida Jeanette an abundance of spare time to talk with neighbors and sip from her medicinal supply. Ida knew quite a bit about the business of everyone in the neighborhood, and freely shared her insights with others over the fence and at Shirley's Beauty Parlor on West Elm. Ida encouraged Eddie Mae to get out more, to be more social.

"I'm sure 'nough thinking it's time you set about finding yourself a feller," she told Eddie Mae. Ida and her acquaintances at Shirley's place have for some time had an informal project under way to introduce her to a suitable male.

The talks with Ida and the visits with the auxiliary women at Freewill Baptist did not fill her need for companionship. There were no kitchen table talks or evening card games with endless circular conversations about the intimate details of personal relationships, family problems, and other topics that women engage in both as entertainment and a way of solving problems. She had never been on a date. She did go to the movie matinee every Saturday at the Crestwood Theatre, watching cowboy movies. Her imaginary friends included Roy Rodgers, Gene Autry, Lash LaRue, the Lone Ranger, Hopalong Cassidy, and the Durango Kid. Even so, she found more interest in the weekly serials that left the hero at the brink of certain disaster, only to escape miraculously the following weekend.

Other than her father, and the movie cowboys, there were no men in Eddie Mae's life. In the first place, she wore too much makeup. The women at church hinted that she really overdid the cosmetics. Print dresses did not become her. Ida Jeanette suggested she might want to consider buying and wearing other than just print dresses. Ida also told her that her appearance might be improved if she would not wear hats with all the flowers on top. Eddie Mae Colvin always wore too much makeup, print dresses and large hats covered with flowers.

On this Saturday evening, like every other for months, Eddie Mae was walking home from the Crestwood. She stopped at the drugstore window where rows and rows of patent medicines were on display. She leaned close to the plate glass and her dark eyes panned the exhibit from left to right. She had tried the pills in most of the small containers a dozen times or more. Not one pill relieved the headaches that plagued her. She dreaded waking in the mornings for fear the headache would return—and it always did. Small Southern towns like Millwood have limited medical service, and each local physician had examined her at one time or another. They found nothing physically wrong and told her so. While diplomatic in their diagnosis, a few suggested the possibility of other problems beyond their ability to treat.

Percy tried often to persuade Eddie Mae to work at Colvin's Mercantile. He envisioned her taking over one day to keep the business going, at least for the loyal neighbors who still stopped by for a few of life's necessities. She brought lunch to the store for him three days a week but did not stay to deal with customers. Answering questions about merchandise and trying to make change at the cash register made her head throb. When he insisted she stay for a time to help and keep him company, dark films crept up around her head and made her feel dizzy. The headache was now unbearable. She simply had to go back home. She needed rest in bed.

Eddie Mae could not remember exactly when the headaches started. It could have been when Mac died. He was the only man besides her father that ever paid any attention to her. She was certain he liked her. He might have been the solution to her life's dilemma; that is, what would happen to her when her father died and what would she do with the store? Mac might have asked her to marry him if he had lived. Mac was the very best grocer in town and everyone knew and admired him. He was a widower with no children. His young wife died shortly after their marriage of some unusual illness and shortly after the opening of their neighborhood grocery. Mac had no interest in another wife. He had a large capacity for work and seemed resigned to running the grocery store, keeping customers happy, and minding his own business.

Every Thursday morning Eddie Mae called in telephone orders for groceries from McCrary's Market. A clerk took down the items and prepared boxes for individual family deliveries. The neighborhood grocery kept a running tab for each family. Percy settled up with Mac at the end of each month. The new man who drove the delivery truck and delivered the weekly order wasn't nearly as nice as Mac. Mac had no business dying and ruining her whole life. If Mac hadn't had that heart attack, she might have had the courage to tell him that she liked him. It would have been easy to do because she made certain she was home on Fridays when he made the deliveries to her street.

The light of the drugstore window seemed brighter as the clouds moved in and the sky grew darker. A fine mist gradually changed to light rain. Eddie Mae pulled her coat collar up around her neck and fixed the flowered hat more firmly to her head. She moved down the sidewalk past the feed store and Martin's Barber Shop, quickening her pace to avoid a coming storm.

At old Mr. Varner's vacant lot she stopped in a dim circle made by the streetlight. "Where can that handkerchief be?" Eddie Mae searched for the thin yellow handkerchief that should be somewhere in her purse. Mac had given it to her one day as he delivered the groceries. She took that to mean that he had feelings for her and it set her mind to all kinds of dreaming about what the little gift could lead to. Her heart beat faster each time she thought about it. She didn't know that almost all Mac's women customers had received thin lady's handkerchiefs that fall in a variety of pastel colors, all resulting from a shipping error from Wasserstein Brothers' Warehouses of New Orleans. When Mac notified them that his store had received the handkerchiefs by mistake, the jobber told him to just keep them as a gift from the supplier in recognition of his past business. Mac had given her the handkerchief the same year he died. Her plans for a more serious relationship turned to severe headaches. If she lost that handkerchief she would surely die.

In the far corner of the vacant lot stood a large cabin tent. In all the many times she had passed this same way she had never seen the tent. It must have been put there during the past week. Eddie Mae never walked to town during the week, people on the street had too much spare time and she couldn't feel at ease. She thought the women were looking at her and she imagined them whispering about her as she passed. On Saturdays she walked directly to the Crestwood Theatre and back with occasional stops at the drugstore for medicine. The few weekday trips to town always made her tired and the headaches grew worse.

The appearance of the tent must signal the start of a new business on the Varner lot. Eddie Mae reached into her handbag for the cream-colored glasses she needed to read any print, large or small. She slipped the thick-lenses spectacles on her nose and slid them in place with her thumb. The light rain was steady now and she held her hand over her eyes to read a painted sign propped against the side of the tent. In bright red letters it read: MADAM GALLOPHILE—MYSTIC OF THE MIND.

Never in her thirty-four years had Eddie Mae had her fortune told. Should she take the risk? What would her father say about spending money this way? Maybe it wouldn't cost that much. She could afford a quarter or so. Surely it would cost more than a quarter. Nobody would ever know if she indulged in this foolish thing.

Eddie Mae walked cautiously across the damp grass toward the tent. She felt something crawling on her ankle, then a slight sting. She reached down with her thumb to squash the tiny insect. The tent was stationed on a wooden platform with the entrance two steps up from the ground. A small bell hung from a flap at the door, begging to be rung. At that moment Eddie Mae considered a change of mind. She wanted to hurry home. Before she could turn around the sound of a motor humming in the back stopped and she heard footsteps. The steps had an irregular pattern that revealed a slight limp. Eddie Mae was frozen in place as the canvas cover opened and a large woman stood just inside the shadows of the tent.

Eddie Mae wanted to run but her knees were too weak to carry her. The woman made a wide sweeping motion with her hand, inviting her to the singular room within. Eddie Mae managed to reach the old-fashioned, high-backed chair that faced the center of a rustic table. Sure enough, a crystal ball sat squarely in the center. Her discomfort was obvious. The fortune-teller smiled and tried to offer assurance that all was well. Both women sat at the table and waited for the sound of a large truck to fade into the distance. The woman wore a colorful shawl-like covering and her fingernails were painted a dark green. A large candle burned in back of her and the scent of incense contributed to the almost surreal atmosphere. The women drew the crystal ball near her and in a thick accent asked, "You wish me to tell your future?"

"How much do you charge, please?"

The women looked at her for a time without expression. "For you, I make no charge."

The aching silence that followed was almost more than Eddie Mae could stand. The common sounds of the street were magnified as she sat with her hand in her lap, daring not move, almost daring not to breathe. The fortune-teller did not turn her eyes from the glistening ball. Eddie Mae imagined she heard whispers round and round in echo fashion—from tongue to tongue and ear to ear.

After what seems an eternity, the strange woman looked up from the table. "I will write your fortune on this paper," she said. "You will put it in your purse and leave it there until you reach your home, then you may look at it and see what."

Eddie Mae thanked the woman, took the paper and quickly deposited it in her small bag. The curiosity gave her legs new life and, once again, she made her way across the lot to the pavement and to the street corner. The drizzle continued and the sky was much darker than when she entered the tent. Eddie Mae had no idea what was written on the paper. Maybe it told of a new life adventure in a big city. Maybe there was a new Mac to be discovered and new friends. Maybe the headaches would go away and she would see a life beyond Millwood and Colvin's Mercantile. Perhaps she would have a new job opportunity and she could buy some new clothes. There was a beautiful new hat in Beall's Department store window with big blue flowers all around the brim.

As Eddie Mae neared the intersection of Martin and Elm, the only thoughts that entered her mind were of the folded paper and of the secret it held. Mr. Mosley, the barber, spoke to her as she reached the corner but she didn't have time to reply. She stopped for a moment to catch her breath, opened the handbag and took out the note. She clutched it tightly in her hand. A large truck loaded with logs from the J. D. Tucker Lumber Company made the turn just as she stepped from the curb. The sound of screeching breaks mingled with shouts from the street. The air filled with a strange odor and Eddie Mae saw many colors before her eyes—a blinding white, fading blue, milky green and then black.

Again the night birds cry. Their cries are deep throated and make an appeal only to heaven. No one knows if heaven hears the tales of hope, love, and loss. The creatures show their faces only in the night. They stand and watch. Perhaps they try to weep. If they weep, it is only for an instant and the tears run quickly to join the raindrops. We will never know if they truly mourn.

The truck came to a sliding stop and the door swung open instantly. Several people ran to the curb. The driver jumped from the cab trying to explain what happened. "She stepped out against the light," he cried. "I didn't see her until it was too late!" A city policeman came running from the drugstore and dispatched an onlooker to call Millwood Hospital for an ambulance.

Mr. Mosley was trying to tell anyone who would listen that he was right at the end of the lot and saw the whole thing happen. "She just walked out in front of the truck," he said. "The driver didn't have a chance to stop!"

Nobody stayed very long. The sky offered a steady drizzle and rain does not lighten the burden of anyone.

The ambulance arrived and the medical attendants determined there was no need to rush. The police officer leaned over the body at the curb. He opened the tightly closed fist and removed a folded piece of paper. He looked at the paper with a quizzical expression.

"Hey, Ralph, what do you figure this means?" he asked the attendant. "This note says, 'You have no future.' "

The Boarder

Potter Ridge, Arkansas
Population: 5,300

Martha Ann Singer thought she heard a knock at the front door. She turned the water off at the sink, listening harder as she dried her hands on the apron at her waist. The second knock was louder. The children, Jeff and Janet, were away at school. Her husband Franklin always skipped breakfast on Fridays in order to open his hardware store early. Customers were eager to buy the necessary materials for weekend projects. She hadn't expected a visitor at this hour of an unusually warm morning in March.

She went to the front to find a man standing at the top of the steps. He held a baseball cap in his hands and beads of perspiration shown at his forehead.

"Yes?" she said. "Can I help you?"

"There was an ad in the paper about a room for rent . . . or am I at the wrong house?"

"Oh no," she answered. "This is the house. Would you like to see the room?"

He nodded as Martha Ann held open the screen door. He wiped his boots on the doormat and stepped inside. As he passed she detected the scent of new leather and tobacco. She showed him the front bedroom, the one she had thoroughly cleaned and carefully prepared before placing the classified ad in the *Potter Ridge Record.* This was the bedroom she and Franklin shared for thirteen years before she announced plans to take in a boarder. Franklin was not taken with the idea of sharing his home with a stranger. Neither did he like giving up his bed. He tried gently to dissuade his wife, protesting the inconvenience and the extra work on her part. Over time he agreed, seeing that Martha Ann had her mind set on it.

The young man was in his late twenties. He had bushy brown hair, blue eyes, and a dark tan. His appearance suggested work that kept him outdoors much of the time. Maybe he worked at the lumber mill she thought, or perhaps with the railroad. The blue denim shirt was nicely laundered and starched, and his khaki pants had neatly pressed seams. He acted shy, slightly nervous, and overly polite.

"We are just opening this room to boarders," she said. "The bathroom is right here but if you don't mind, it has to be shared with our nine-year-old son, Jeff."

The young man stepped into the room and looked around. Saying nothing he opened the door to the bath and looked in.

"I am Martha Ann Singer." She held out her hand. "And your name?"

"James Tyler," he answered, "but everyone just calls me Jim."

"Well, Jim," she said, "I should let you know the room is $25 a month, and I come in to clean and do the sheets once a week. You must be new to Potter Ridge. Are you working at the sawmill?"

Jim explained that he was employed with a road construction company out of Fort Smith. The company had just received a contract from the Arkansas Department of Highways to repair several bridges in the western part of Mayford County. He didn't have need for a car he said, since he enjoyed walking the few blocks from the town square. He took his meals at the Red Rooster Restaurant and met the other workers there each morning for breakfast and the day's assignments. Most of the other construction employees had rooms at The Webster, the town's only hotel located just across the street from the Red Rooster and next door to the First National Bank of Potter Ridge. Jim had been staying at The Webster but was eager to find more affordable accommodations. He told her the room would do fine and he would like to move in as soon as possible.

That's how Martha Ann took in a boarder, hoping to add extra income for the family at a time when funds were short. Most families in small Southern towns managed to get by in the 1940s, shaking off the effects of the war and hoping the returning service men would help the economy grow. Located in the northeast part of the state and not far from the Mississippi River, Potter Ridge is just south of the Missouri state line. Small towns did not recover from the war years as quickly as Memphis or St. Louis. The merchants and farm families of the region struggled to stay above the poverty line.

Franklin and Martha Ann graduated in the Potter Ridge High School class of 1935 and married shortly afterwards. They had been sweethearts during their junior and senior years, with marriage the understood next step in their relationship. She was good at bookkeeping and English, earning class honors in both subjects. She sang in the school chorus and passed up opportunities to try out for cheerleader. She was an outgoing girl but not popular with the in crowd. Her father and mother never talked with her about college. Neither parent had a post-secondary education and saw little value in spending that kind of money when jobs were available in Memphis or Little Rock, if not right there in Potter Ridge. Martha Ann was expected to get married and start having children.

Franklin's parents were farmers, living on eighty acres just south of town. He was an average student, active in the 4-H Club and played offensive tackle on the high school football team. His part-time job after school and on Saturdays at Simpson's Hardware didn't leave much time for extra activities. Martha Ann could not remember knowing him when he had not worked at the hardware. Mr. Simpson offered him a full-time job right after high school and Franklin never considered college

Jim Tyler arrived back at the Singers' that evening with a cardboard suitcase and small canvas bag. He settled into the front bedroom and became Martha Ann's new charge.

"Are you comfortable in there?" she asked the first time he emerged to have a smoke.

"Yes, ma'am," he answered, offering no more as he descended the steps and headed cross the yard toward the large magnolia tree that anchored the property to the east.

"Let me know if you need more towels," she said.

"Yes, ma'am," was his only response.

That became the pattern of their relationship: landlord and boarder. She tried to be friendly and attempted light conversation at every meeting. He was not unpleasant but was clearly intent on keeping to himself. While the boarder had little to say to Martha Ann, Franklin or Janet, he seemed much more comfortable with Jeff. Jeff was outgoing and talkative, and conversation with strangers came easy to him. Janet, Jeff's older sister by two years, was in the process of discovering boys and spent endless time in her room primping and changing clothes. She was interested primarily in herself, certainly not the boarder.

After supper, just as the sun angled toward the smoke stack at the East Arkansas Lumber Company, Jeff would join Jim at the side porch. He was fascinated by Jim's evening ritual of rolling a smoke. Jim pulled a package of cigarette papers and a small string bag of tobacco from his shirt pocket. He carefully balanced a thin white rectangle of paper in his left hand, creating a cradle between his thumb and index finger. With the tobacco pouch in his right hand, Jim pulled open the bag with the string in his teeth. After carefully pouring an even row of tobacco in the paper cradle, he reversed the process, pulling the string bag closed with his teeth and placing both the paper and tobacco back in his pocket. Jim then ran his tongue along the outer edge of the paper, dampening the tissue. He folded the homemade cigarette into place. It was a delicate balancing act. Jeff watched this with great interest, assuming he would be trying the same thing when older.

They talked about the construction work and Jim asked questions about school. Jeff's passion was basketball and he would soon be able to try out for the junior varsity squad at Potter Ridge High. Jeff was curious about Jim's knowledge of sports and asked questions about his experiences. Jim managed to sidestep each question about his past, always turning the discussion back to Jeff.

Five years after Martha Ann and Franklin married, Wallace B. Simpson died of a heart attack. He had not been sick a day in his life and since birth had never spent a night in a hospital. No one in the town of Potter Ridge was prepared for Mr. Simpson's death. The hardware was a permanent fixture at the southwest corner of the town square. With Mr. Simpson's death, Franklin was uncertain about his future and prospects for the store. He knew more than anyone except Mr. Simpson about the products and prices, and had almost mastered the inventory ordering system. Mr. Simpson went out of his way to show him his methods for scheduling purchases, stocking items, and tracking his profits. He feared all that extra study and effort could go for nothing.

The *Potter Ridge Record* carried Mr. Simpson's obituary on the front page:

> *Wallace B. Simpson, age 74, died Friday, April 20, 1947, at his home on West Broad Street. Mr. Simpson was the owner and manager of Simpson's Hardware. He was born on August 30, 1867 in Helena, the son of Delbert and Pearl Simpson. He is survived by his wife, Rachel Hunt Simpson of the home; two daughters, Elizabeth Daniels of Fort Smith, Ark., and Margaret Ann Barber of Fenton, Mo.; one sister, Maybell Armond Smith, of Chicago, Ill.; and four grandchildren.*

Martha Ann signed the guest book as they entered the church. This was the first time she and Franklin had attended a funeral as a couple. She had gone with her parents to her aunt Lou Ann Foster's funeral over in Forrest City when she was a senior in high school. The time and the circumstances here were much different. Wallace Simpson was not supposed to die. He did not act his age, was active in the store, his church and the community. As the founder and first president of the Potter Ridge Economic Council he had worked to bring new industry to the county, and more customers to his hardware. Mr. Simpson was not only her husband's boss, but represented a stabilizing force for small business owners in the county and in an otherwise uncertain community economy.

The hardware remained closed for two days after the funeral and was reopened by Franklin the following Thursday. He tried to keep things going until Mrs. Simpson decided what she wanted to do. She would now be the sole owner and decision maker. Franklin thought she would probably want to sell the store since she had never been personally involved in the business. He only hoped he could stay on with any new owner long enough to rethink his own plans, but knew that would be an uncertainty. He had no other job prospects and retail opportunities in small town Potter Ridge were limited.

With his knowledge of, and experience in, the hardware business, Franklin began developing a plan for checking into jobs at larger hardware firms in West Memphis, Helena and Forrest City.

The week following the funeral, Rachel Simpson called Franklin and asked him to come by her home that evening after closing. So, he thought, this would be it! This would be the somber meeting where she would thank him for his years of service and announce plans for selling or simply closing the establishment. In all the years he had worked for Mr. Simpson, this was the first time he had ever been invited to their home. The two-story colonial on West Broad Street was attractive and well-kept, reflecting the handiwork of a hardware owner who knew how to use the tools of his trade. The living room was furnished with taste and Mrs. Simpson ushered Franklin into the parlor where coffee and freshly baked cookies awaited.

"Wallace and I talked about you and your work about three months before he died," she told him. "He was very proud of the way you learned the business and took on extra responsibility."

"Thank you, Mrs. Simpson," he said. "That was nice of him."

"Please call me Rachel," she answered. "It looks as if we may be partners . . . that is, if you want to continue on at the store."

"Well, certainly," he said. "I do . . . I don't really know any other business."

"Wallace talked about how he might find a way one day for you to have some ownership in the business. He was working with Clyde Evans at First National, checking into some financial arrangement before he said anything to you."

"That would be very nice," he answered, "but I never thought that would be possible."

"Well, we can still work that out over time, but for now I want to promote you to manager of the store and rely on you to just take over and run the business."

"I can do that, Mrs. Simpson . . . I mean Rachel . . . because he had just finished teaching me how to plan and manage the inventory."

"I'm pleased to hear that." She smiled. "And that would mean a nice increase in income. How about we raise your salary to $450 a month?"

"I'll need to hire some help, if that's all right with you?" he ventured. "It would be very hard to keep things going just by myself."

"Certainly," she said. "You just take over and do what you need to do to run the business. And it would also be nice if we actually made a profit."

Franklin took on the additional duties associated with full responsibility for the hardware and began searching for a full-time employee as well as part-time help. He also knew that $450 a month with a wife and children to support left little room for building equity in a business.

Martha Ann was pleased with the news for Franklin's sake, even though she secretly hoped he would be more ambitious in seeking a different job and more compensation. She would not be opposed to leaving Potter Ridge, say moving to Memphis, Little Rock, or even St. Louis. The raise in salary did not change her thoughts about renting out the front bedroom and the need for additional income.

The first few weeks with a new boarder went by without incident and Jim Tyler settled into a routine of coming and going, with very little contact with the Singer family. Still, neighbors began to talk. Wilma Reynolds, in particular, was intensely interested in the arrangement. She lived in the corner house across the street from the Singers and made no attempt to be friendly with anyone on the block. Her husband drove a log truck for the Mayford Lumber Company and was away much of the time. She found a way to bring up the subject of the new Singer tenant during her weekly trip to Hazel's Cut & Curl Salon. Every Thursday morning she had a standing appointment for a wash and set, making certain she left time for a weekly supply of beauty parlor gossip.

"What do you suppose brought Martha Anne to the point of taking on a boarder?" she asked no one in particular. "Since Franklin was made manager of the hardware, I thought they wouldn't need more income."

"It isn't unusual for people to rent out extra bedrooms these days," said Sandra Sue Hamaker, who was waiting for a particular hairdresser to be free. "My sister over in Cotton Plant has a boarder."

Wilma had more to say. "If I was Franklin I don't think I would like the idea of a younger man in the house alone with my wife."

"The man works during the day," observed Maribell Jacobs from under the hair dryer. "I wouldn't go 'round spreading rumors about the boarder and Martha Ann!"

"I wasn't spreading no rumor," she quickly defended. "I was just asking the question."

The Cut & Curl conversation traveled on at that pace for a time before someone brought up Margaret Rider's new red Ford convertible. The discussion then took an oblique left turn toward fancy automobiles. Still, the idea of something untoward between Martha Ann and the boarder had been introduced into the beauty shop arena. Margaret said she had heard talk about it among the tellers and clerks at the First National Bank. Others in the neighborhood were curious about the appearance of the man but had not talked about it with others on the block.

On this particular morning, Martha Ann was having troubles with her daughter. Janet was trying out for a part in the sophomore class one-act play *A Lovely Time for Living.* She was in serious pursuit of the lead and was not at all happy with the outfit her mother suggested. She had to be dressed exactly right to influence Miss Thurman, the speech and English teacher directing this year's production. The wardrobe conflict between Martha Ann and Janet disrupted breakfast, so much so that Franklin and Jeff excused themselves early, not the least bit interested in any spat over clothing or appearances.

When the disagreement was settled, with Janet changing outfits a third time, Martha Ann poured herself a second cup of coffee and sat down at the kitchen table to read. The *Potter Ridge Record* carried little national or state news, and Martha Ann had heard details of the local stories at the Laundromat or grocery weeks before they appeared in print. Her mind wandered to the boarder, his shy and unsocial behavior, and the faraway look in his eyes. The arrangement was working to her satisfaction, but not as comfortable as she had imagined. Several of their friends had asked questions about the boarder, a bit nosey she thought, but not unusual for a small community where everyone knew everyone. She did not, however, find the tone of their inquiries curious.

She folded the morning newspaper and put it aside, staring at the coffee cup in front of her. Mary Anne Singer was weary. Not weary in the sense that she had physical problems, maybe just bored or unfulfilled. She loved Franklin very much and the children made their marriage complete. Still, there was an ingrained monotony to her world, something that had been closing in for months. She thought she should be happy, married with two children and a husband with a respectable job in their hometown. Still, something was missing. What if she had gone on to Arkansas State at Jonesboro and worked on a degree in liberal arts? What if she had become a teacher?

Jeff was in fifth grade at the nearby elementary school. Janet was a popular member of Potter Ridge sophomore class. Martha Ann could do her home chores in no time. She had no interest in the neighborhood canasta club. While the gossip at Hazel's Cut & Curl was entertaining, it could not fill the nagging void she felt, a need for something more worthy to occupy her thoughts and time. It would be wonderful to have enough extra income to take a nice trip every year, say to New York City or Miami, Florida. They had planned a summer vacation on the Mississippi Gulf Coast once, with reservations at a resort on Santa

Rosa Island. The trip was canceled at the last minute when the one full-time assistant at Simpson's Hardware got sick.

Franklin went to the store every morning without complaint, earning a modest living for his family. *He is a good man,* she thought. *He works very hard to take care of me and the children, and he is doing the best he can with what he knows.* Earlier in their marriage she had thoughts about looking for a job outside the home when Jeff and Janet were old enough to be in school. If only she had gone on to college. There weren't many jobs available in town that she could feel comfortable with. That's why she insisted on transforming the front bedroom for a boarder. She hadn't thought about any lodging permits required for taking in boarders, fire codes, business fees, or any accounting practices necessary for tax purposes. In Potter Ridge, these issues were not high priority items with city officials.

As the end of April arrived, the boarder's first full month in the front bedroom, he approached Martha Ann with a request.

"I had lots of start-up expenses when I came to town," he told her. "Would it be okay for me to pay two month's rent when I get my next month's paycheck?"

"I suppose so," she answered, taken aback and unable to think clearly how to respond. The $25 due had already been allocated in her mind: a school fund to help with clothes and supplies for the following year and a few dollars put aside every month for the vacation fund.

"I will need two full month's payments next time." She tried to sound stern with the statement but it didn't really come off as she had intended. She so wanted to see New York City, and Radio City Music Hall, and the Rockettes, and the Statue of Liberty. She would just have to wait to get that started next month when the $50 came in.

"Thank you, ma'am," he said. "I appreciate it." Jim offered nothing more, turned into the front bedroom and closed the door behind him.

The following Friday Martha Ann was cleaning the room, taking the boarder's sheets to laundry, when she discovered an odor in or near the chest of drawers. She was reluctant to explore because she did not want to intrude on his belongings, but something was not right in that corner of the room.

She followed her nose to the bottom draw and slowly pulled it open. A scent rose from the dresser and filled the room. The drawer was empty except for open potted meat and Vienna sausage cans. There were also empty saltine cracker boxes. An army of ants had set up camp there and was feasting on the remnants of potted meat and cracker crumbs. She hurriedly cleaned out the mess and scrubbed the drawer.

If she said something to Jim he would know she had been doing more than dusting and laundry. She decided to simply let it go, not even mentioning it to Franklin. That would again bring into question the wisdom of taking in a boarder in the first place.

Franklin's new assistant at Simpson's Hardware was working out fine, to the point where he did not have to spend as much time directly with customers. That allowed him to pursue an idea involving the offer of unfinished furniture in an area at the rear of the hardware. He discussed this with Mrs. Simpson and she encouraged him to do what he thought best. Since his taking over management, the business had gradually moved from a breakeven to a modest profit position.

After weeks of correspondence and more than a few phone calls to St. Louis, Franklin arranged for samples from the Black Jack Wood Products Company to be shipped to Potter Ridge. He even fashioned an advertisement to run in the *Potter Ridge Record* announcing the new line. There were unfinished bookcases, dinette tables and chairs, children's furniture pieces and several all-purpose cabinets.

With a new sign in the window and the ad in the newspaper, Franklin was sure folks would drop in for a look with the possibility of purchasing a few hardware items on the way out even if they didn't buy unfinished furniture. The product addition was not a resounding success. After two weeks of the merchandise on display, only Elizabeth Ann Rodney, the high school English teacher, had purchased one bookcase for her kitchen. She allowed as how her collection of cookbooks was getting completely out of hand.

The following Friday, Martha Ann was again taking sheets and bedding from the boarder's room when she saw an assortment of magazines on the floor near the head of the bed. She let them go until she retuned to sweep and dust the room. A second look gave her a start. The cover photo of the magazine on top was of a young woman with no clothes on, smiling as she displayed a set of ample breasts. Martha Ann picked up the magazines and began thumbing through the stack. They were full of photos unlike anything she had ever seen, certainly not anything they would ever permit in their home. The articles had titles that made her blush, and she couldn't imagine any establishment in Potter Ridge selling such publications.

The magazine and newspaper racks at Phillip's Drug Store and Carry's Soda Fountain carried the *Arkansas Gazette*, *Arkansas Democra*t and *Memphis Appeal*. There were publications such as *Ladies Home Journal*, *Sportsman*, *Popular Mechanics,* and the *Saturday Evening Post*. No girlie magazines were to be found in any reputable establishment downtown. Where could James Tyler have gotten them?

Martha Ann didn't want to leave the magazines in the room. Still, they did not belong to her and she was uncertain as to how to handle the situation. She hoped against hope that the boarder had not shown such material to Jeff. She turned the magazines upside down and placed them back under the bed in a neat stack. She said nothing about them to the boarder or to her husband.

One morning in late May the telephone rang as Martha Ann was dressing for a trip to the grocery. The caller identified himself as Ralph Douglas, project manager for the Fort Smith construction company.

"I understand that Jim Tyler has a room at your place," he said.

"Yes, he does," she answered. "Is something wrong?"

"I don't know," he responded. "This is the second day in a row he hasn't shown up for work. I just thought he might be sick, or something."

She told him she had not seen Jim recently, but that was not unusual. Mr. Douglas stayed on the phone while Martha Ann checked his room. She knocked on the bedroom door and called his name. There was no answer. She knocked a second time then eased open the door. There she discovered drawers to the dresser hanging open, the closet was empty and the boarder's suitcase and canvas bag were missing. Jim Tyler was gone!

She retuned to the phone and explained the circumstance to Mr. Douglas. He said he would contact the company headquarters and talk with the Potter Ridge police. He gave her a telephone number and asked her to call if Jim showed up, suggesting the possibility of foul play. They both were puzzled by his disappearance.

Martha Ann could not continue with her plans for the day. She did not know what to do, sitting at the kitchen table and imagining the worse. Tyler owed her $50 and had simply skipped out. She had been counting on that money as clear evidence to Franklin that she had done the right thing by opening their home to a boarder. Now she felt foolish, thinking about all that extra effort to prepare the front bedroom, the cost of an ad in the classifieds, and the weekly cleaning and laundry. She wanted to cry but couldn't. She just felt empty and used. How could she break this news to Franklin?

That night at the supper table she tried more than once to tell him, always changing her mind. It was Franklin who first brought up the subject.

"I had a visit at the store today from Sheriff Troy Adkins," he said. "He came by to ask several questions about your boarder."

Her breath tightened. "What questions?"

"Troy said he had a call from Beaumont, Texas. Seems that law officers there were searching for a man who had violated his parole about seven months ago, and they had some indication he might be in this area."

"Was it our boarder?" she asked.

"They don't know, but he was about the same age and description as Tyler."

She collected her thoughts in silence. Franklin returned to his meatloaf and mashed potatoes. While she wasn't certain she wanted to know, she asked anyway: "The person they are looking for . . . what crime had he been convicted of anyway?"

"I believe Troy mentioned armed robbery."

The next day Martha Ann removed the front bedroom bedding and deposited it in a Dumpster behind Rodden's supermarket. She gave the room a thorough cleaning and bought new sheets and pillowcases. Without consultation, she moved her clothes and Franklin's back into the front room chest of draws and closet. She would tell Franklin about the missing boarder when he came home from work that evening. In the meantime, she would have to come up with a new scheme for additional income, and an eventual trip to New York, or Miami. One day she would see the ocean, the Rockettes, the Statue of Liberty and Empire State Building.

The Grace Vespers Committee

Bradford, Missouri
Population: 11,480

They arrived within minutes of each other, in time for the regular morning billiards game in the basement recreation room at the Grace Presbyterian Church. On this particular Wednesday, Carlton, Joe Allen and W. T. had more serious things to talk about. The cue stick remained cradled in the rack and the balls in the pockets.

Joe Allen cleaned the coffeepot while Carlton opened a new can of Folger's regular blend. W. T. was in an agitated state, pacing back and forth, in no mood for the usual small talk.

"I've seen about as much as I can stand," said W. T. "I'm ready to do something myself!" He was red in the face and his anger was near the surface with veins visible above his collar.

"We have to stay calm," offered Joe Allen. "No need to do anything irrational."

"Irrational hell," Carlton chimed in. "Wouldn't you call beating up on a woman and little kid irrational? The city cops around here are totally worthless. Maybe it's time we tried a few vigilante tactics."

The church recreation room had become a regular meeting place for the trio, all adjusting to new schedules and different lives, circumstances associated with the early years of retirement. While they had not been close acquaintances during working careers, idle time and similar interests produced new friendships and a special camaraderie.

The recreation room was open to church members and available as a place to meet for coffee and conversation. The pool game was just an excuse. None of them was particularly skilled with the cue stick and they made no effort toward improving. The Wednesday sessions were mostly exchanges of information and ideas about the latest newspaper coverage of local politics and government officials in Jefferson City or the nation's capital. They all had opinions about the articles they read in the *Bradford Telegraph* and *St. Louis Post-Dispatch.*

Joe Allen and Nancy Jean Crawford

Joe Allen Crawford had grown up in Bradford, a town of 11,000 located in the southeast corner of Missouri. He stood tall and slightly bowlegged in the 1948 graduating class at Bradford High. Shortly afterwards he joined the Navy. No one in his farm family had been to college and the idea of post-secondary education had not crossed his mind. His uncle Clyde from Little Rock had been in the Navy, coming back home with a head full of stories about his adventures at sea, interesting ports of call, unusual people and special memories. Joe had been thinking about the Navy since junior high.

After basic training at the Great Lakes Naval Training Center near Chicago, and tours in Norfolk and Guantanamo Bay, Joe Allen was released from active duty and returned to Bradford. He found work quickly in the flooring mill, working his way eventually to the head estimator position. He made a modest but decent salary, and the job included medical benefits and a pension plan. His high school sweetheart, Nancy Jean McGraw, passed up college as well to work as a clerk in the ladies wear department of Steward's Mercantile, the only decent clothing store in Bradford. Joe Allen and Nancy Jean were married a year later. They had no children, but treated their dog Biscuit as more than a pet. Biscuit wanted for nothing, and was in reality their only child.

Joe Allen and Nancy were huge baseball fans. They attended every home game of the Bradford Pilots, a semipro team of the Mid-States League. They were also season ticket holders for the major home games of the St. Louis Cardinals, traveling often to the Gateway City for long weekends of baseball and pampering at the Marriott Pavilion Hotel just across the street from Busch Stadium.

Carlton W. and Martha Lou Crews

Carlton W. Crews lived on Baker Avenue, two blocks east of the church. He was always first to arrive for their Wednesday pool games, taking pride in having the coffee ready and the balls racked. That was the order of his life: planning ahead, establishing a list of tasks, and accomplishing them on time and in order. Accountants are often smitten with those traits. Carlton earned a degree in accounting at Arkansas State, Jonesboro, completing all the requirements for his CPA credentials two years later. He returned to Bradford and established his own accounting firm. Business was a struggle in the early years. He was smart but young. Older men had accumulated and controlled the significant wealth of the region, the kind of assets that benefit from professional accounting services. Carlton persisted and over time he gained enough clients to keep the doors open, hire a secretary-clerk, and eventually purchase his own office space.

The first secretary he hired answered an ad in the *Bradford Telegraph*. The want ad called for "a person with an outgoing personality, good bookkeeping and typing skills." Carlton thought his business could benefit from someone at ease on the telephone and comfortable dealing with business people such as bankers, small business owners and merchants. Martha Lou Saunders was the first and only one to answer his ad. She was six years younger than Carlton, a shapely girl with limpid blue eyes and a casual mane of ash-blond hair. She had quick wit and a ready smile. He hired her on the first interview, but knew right away there would be a problem. He tried to maintain their relationship on a strict business basis, but came to understand rather quickly that the boss-employee arrangement would not work. Carlton fell in love with Martha Lou during their first week together. They were soon completing the workday with an early evening ritual at The Bradford Café, sharing stories about their lives, hopes, dreams and aspirations over coffee and pecan pie. Carlton knew early on she was the companion he wanted for life. He proposed marriage eighteen months later and the couple honeymooned in New Orleans, spending a glorious week at the Royal Sonesta Hotel near the corner of Bourbon and Conti.

The Crews had one child, a daughter they named Charlotte. She was a delight to her dad and a girlfriend to her mother. Charlotte breezed through Bradford High and headed for St. Louis and Webster University. Her degree in political science led to a staff job in the Department of Labor in Washington, D.C. The Crews were very proud of their daughter and worried about her living alone in a big city.

Over a period of twenty-nine years Carlton had established a sound accounting business, eventually hiring a partner and working for clients throughout the Missouri Boot Heel. His partner bought him out and Carlton retired with few hobbies and no plan for his remaining years. His friendship with Joe Allen and W. T., their occasional fishing trips to Feather Point Lake, Bradford Pilots baseball games, and the Wednesday morning coffee and pool outings provided a diversion from the monotony of small-town existence.

William T. and Mary Ann Pennington

William Tucker Pennington, known by all as W. T., had a daughter Sue Ellen and grandson Tuck. He retired from the U.S. Postal Service after thirty-two years, starting as a rural carrier and ending his career as assistant postmaster. His wife Mary Ann died of cancer in her mid-forties and W. T. devoted his energies to raising Sue Ellen and seeing her through Southeast Missouri State. She was an English major with an early education minor. Her plans to teach were sidetracked by marriage. Now Sue Ellen and little Tuck were in harm's way.

By now W. T.'s retirement buddies Joe Allen and Carlton knew the story well. W. T.'s son-in-law was a well-known Bradford attorney with ties to city hall. John Charles Abbington was a popular man about town, son of Robert Elsworth Abbington, retired CEO and president of the Bradford Merchants & Planters Bank. That didn't prevent John Charles from occasional excesses with sour mash, after which his disposition changed. He grew mean and nasty, always taking his problems out on his wife, slapping her around, calling her names and leaving her so battered and bruised that she didn't dare show herself in public for days afterwards.

The abuse started two years before. He hit her only once after returning from an office Christmas party where he had overindulged. This was the first time she had seen such behavior and the first time he had struck her in five years of marriage. She was shocked, hurt and embarrassed. However, she let it all pass, attributing it to the season and the alcohol. She didn't tell anyone, not even her closest girlfriends. The embarrassment was too great. Her husband, after all, was one of the town's leading attorneys. Who would believe such a story?

After majoring in business administration at Southeastern Missouri State, John Charles worked for a time in his father's bank. He wasn't cut out for banking, found it boring, confining and far too routine. He grew restless, choosing to move to St. Louis to try his hand at law school. His grades were adequate and his connections such that St. Louis University Law School accepted his application.

He lived in an apartment in the Central West End, studied just enough to get by, and spent many leisure hours in the clubs and bars of Laclede's Landing near the Mississippi River. It was in those establishments and during those late night hours that he took an unusual liking to strong drink.

When he returned to Bradford and opened his own law practice, business came to him naturally. His father steered clients his way from the bank and soon he had to add additional lawyers and clerical staff. His marriage to Sue Ellen Pennington was no surprise. They were both popular in high school and had dated on and off through both their junior and senior years.

The pattern was classic: He was always appropriately sorry after sobering up, always promising this was the last time, and assuring her that she and the boy were the loves of his life. She wanted to believe him, needed to believe him, and tried very hard to keep their marriage alive. Weeks, even months went by and their lives settled into a routine of work and attention to the activities of little Tuck. During this latest incident, however, he had roughed her up badly, but that was not the least of it. This time he had also knocked little Tuck against a table, scaring him to death and creating a huge red welt on his left cheek.

Bradford was not the kind of town where neighbors make trouble. Sue Ellen dropped their son off at Sunday school and made up an excuse for missing two church services in a row. Her friends were suspicious. John Charles blustered his way through the law work and did not miss regular coffee sessions at the bank. He could be charming; he could be intimidating. He had rather strong opinions about most political issues in the region and state, freely sharing them with a cadre of the town's professionals and merchants gathered at the bank each weekday morning for coffee and conversation. Several members of the morning coffee klatch did not welcome his abrasive style but tolerated the behavior in deference to his father. For the most part Bradford life had a predictable, satisfying sameness.

"Martha Lou and I have been married almost forty years," said Carlton. "I ain't never once considered even the possibility of hitting that woman!"

He sat down on a straight-backed metal chair near the door and placed his head in his hands. "When you got a good, lovin' woman in your life, you better treat her right. Treat her with respect!" After a long pause he added, "Your daughter is a good, loving woman W. T."

"What kind of man would beat up on a woman like that?" W. T. spoke as he walked to the coffeepot and poured a cup. His offering was more of a statement than a question.

"I thought I knew John Charles," he said. "He always was a bit cocky, a little too sure of himself, but he was also smart as hell. He just got by in school, making decent grades without studying. I never expected he would do this to Sue Ellen, and certainly not little Tuck. This time I believe he has crossed the line. I'm not just disappointed any more. This time I'm spitting mad!"

On two other occasions when he had gotten out of line, the Bradford police were notified. A young officer came over and rang the doorbell. John Charles told him all was well, no need to worry; there was simply a misunderstanding.

"Thank you for coming by," he told the young officer. "I'm very impressed with your attention to detail. If there had actually been trouble here, I would be reassured by your responding so quickly. I'll make sure to mention that next time I am working a case with Chief Malone."

"Thank you, sir," the officer said with a smile. He was understanding and certainly not eager to be further involved with the banker's son. No reports were ever filed.

Carlton and Joe each poured a steaming cup of coffee and sat down. They were visualizing the beating of W. T.'s daughter and the roughing up of little Tuck. Carlton's vigilante remark hung heavy in the morning air.

W. T. paced from one end of the pool table to the other. The three remained silent, each with personal thoughts about the issue. W. T. stopped and stared out the window toward the post office. He was working on an idea.

"What would you think about forming a special Grace Vespers Committee to deal with unusual circumstances around this county?" he asked.

"What kind of committee?" asked Joe Allen.

"What special circumstances?" chimed in Carlton.

"I was thinking we might just form a new committee to solve a few problems the worthless Bradford police ignore. We could hold vespers with a few people around here who could use a lesson or two delivered in the woodshed style, something my grandpa used to call a come-to-Jesus meeting.'"

Carlton and Joe Allen looked at each other without speaking. It was clear W. T. had his son-in-law in mind and they were being enlisted as assistant instructors. That's how the unofficial Grace Vespers Committee was formed. They abandoned the pool game entirely and set about discussing what role the alliance might play, identifying several Bradford citizens who could do with some remedial training in old-fashioned Southern manners.

Men who have worked a lifetime, provided for themselves and their families, saved a reasonable amount of what they earned, and now enjoy a comfortable retirement, develop a more relaxed view of the universe. They had less to learn the hard way, and their intolerance for misbehavior was fueled by a seasoned sense of justice. At this time of life their coffee talk was more thoughtful, less strident, with a less complicated vision of the difference in good and bad, right and wrong.

While all three men were in their mid-seventies, they were active and in good health. They worked in their yards, mowing lawns, trimming trees and hauling mulch for flower beds and gardens. They fished at Feather Point Lake, trolling for white perch, which they called crappie. Over the several years of retirement they had become close friends, the kind of friends who look out for you and lend a hand without your even having to ask.

So, Joe Allen, Carlton, and W. T. formed an alliance of sorts, calling it the Grace Vespers Committee. While they had no special plan of action, they were in agreement about a certain need in the Bradford community. The larger question was: Could three old men actually make a difference, even if it required a certain amount of physical intimidation?

The Wednesday morning conversations in the church basement took on a deeper, more philosophical tone over the next two weeks. The frustration and anger felt by W. T., Carlton, and Joe Allen as a result of the continued mistreatment of W. T.'s daughter and grandson gave way to an exploration of their most personal life experiences, questioning each other about the rationale behind this plan. What right did they have as mere citizens of Bradford to take the law into their own hands, even if the initial goal was to avenge the hostile treatment of a woman and child? They tested their own motives and their resolve to personal involvement, even if it was unorthodox to the point of justice in the form of hostile antagonism.

The pool cues remained in the rack and the sessions lasted longer into the morning. The trio talked about the intransigence of their local government, of politicians who come and go while problems continue to plague and persist. The ineffective, almost somnambulant, Bradford police department was comical in a way, consisting of a handful of small-time, politically appointed Barney Fifes. They were reprehensibly inept, incapable of contending with bullies of any ilk. They viewed the department as simply a gang of rednecks masquerading as law enforcement.

The scope of the conversations, the probing for a deeper understanding of the values of each led to an unusual bonding. Their discussions resulted in a satisfying conclusion, a philosophy central to the Grace Vespers Committee. In the seventh decade of their lives, there came a time when a true conscience could tolerate no more compromise; when for their self-respect, and for that of their children and grandchildren, they would risk their own futures to do what they firmly thought needed to be done.

The decision was to move ahead with the unauthorized committee of three and to no longer hesitate because of any personal consequence. The next step was to schedule a few "vesper services" for individuals who required extralegal lessons in justice.

The following Wednesday morning, as early fall weather made the air crisp and clean, they met at the church basement to map out their initial step.

"John Charles plays poker on Wednesday nights at the VFW hut," said W. T. "He doesn't usually leave there until around midnight, and by then he has put away several bourbons."

Carlton suggested the trio might just plan a visit when John Charles returned to the parking lot after his VFW evening.

"What if there is a big fight?" questioned Joe Allen. "Are we ready for dealing with that?"

"I'm ready," said W. T. "If it comes to that I can be escorted away by either the police or pallbearers."

The plan was to confront John Charles the following week as he left the poker game. He would be challenged about the treatment of his wife and child, and he would receive an ultimatum about the consequence of any continued abusive behavior. If stronger measures were required, he would be roughed up a bit.

They met in the church basement the following Wednesday morning, poured hot coffee and sat quietly for a time. The committee was now operational. They ignored the pool table and moved from small talk to more reflective matters. During the many months that formed their companionship, none of the talk was introspective and they did not share specifics about marriages, their children, or particular philosophies about life. This morning was different. They talked about the Bradford they grew up in during the 1930s and '40s, the good-old-days virtue and lives of unimaginable simplicity. The young families of the region, represented at the extreme by son-in-law John Charles Abbington, were more active, far more mobile, influenced by an information-driven culture, and less concerned about community. The behavior of the community had changed and, to their way of thinking, not for the better. The conversation mellowed and they agreed, with a sense of some embarrassment, that nostalgic moralists are almost always correct.

Carlton, the most widely read of the trio, suggested that virtues always look better in retrospect. While the more sobering thoughts caused some doubt about their ploy, the thoughts of more harm to Sue Ellen and Tuck led them to agree on a time to meet that evening for their first confrontation.

Joe Allen, who had coached youth baseball for the Bradford Babe Ruth League, brought along a bungee bat. W. T. retrieved a large tire iron from his pickup truck, and Carlton found several feet of chain in the back of his garage. They felt a bit uncomfortable but excited. If the meeting resulted in a physical confrontation, they would be ready. This was to be an important evening.

Joe Allen volunteered to pick up the others about a half hour before midnight. W. T. and Carlton were both waiting in their driveways when he arrived. They drove halfway around the town square and down South Main to the VFW hut. Joe Allen spotted John Charles' Buick Regal and parked nearby. He turned off the lights and they waited. Between 11:45 P.M. and midnight, as if on cue, John Charles was the first to emerge from the poker game, walking with a deliberate gait toward his car. His steps were sure and direct, displaying no sign of the effects of alcohol.

The truck doors opened simultaneously and members of the Grace Vespers Committee stepped out. W. T. spoke first.

"We need to talk with you about something very serious, John Charles."

"What are you fellows doing out so late," he said with a smile. "Shouldn't you be home in bed by now?"

W. T. continued, "This isn't a joking matter. We need to talk with you about your treatment of Sue Ellen and little Tuck."

The four men stood in a semicircle. John Charles saw the bat, chain and tire iron. The committee waited for him to respond. The silence that followed was awkward. John Charles did not react as they had expected. His shoulders slumped and he took a deep breath, letting the air out slowly.

"I'm afraid y'all are a little late," he said. "I've already been scolded in a much tougher way than you could ever deliver."

"What do you mean?" said Carlton.

"I wish you would have been here several weeks ago with you bats and stuff, and I wish you had beat some sense into me. Now it's too late."

John Charles had a pained look on his face and he appeared near tears. W. T. had never seen this behavior in his son-in-law and was confused by it.

"I guess you hadn't heard the news, Pop. Sue Ellen had divorce papers issued on Monday. She and Tuck are in St. Louis staying with one of her old sorority sisters."

"I didn't know anything about it," said W. T.

"She was probably too embarrassed to tell anybody," he said. "I tried to talk with her on the phone but she was dead serious about leaving me. I've screwed up bad and I'm about to lose the two most important people in my life."

There was another period of silence. The three retirees could not look at each other. They felt awkward and out of place. Others begin to leave the VFW hut and several looked over at the group with questioning glances.

Joe Allen broke the silence. "We feel bad for you and Sue Ellen," he said. "We were also mad as hell about how she and the little Tuck have been treated, and we wanted to discuss that with you."

"I'm glad you fellows actually give a damn!" replied John Charles. "I know I have a problem with the booze, and I have to do something about it. In fact, I'll be attending AA meetings starting next week. If I can get straightened out, maybe I can fix things with my family."

W. T.'s tone of voice and demeanor changed instantly. "What can we do to help?"

"When you talk to Sue Ellen, please tell her I am very sorry for what I did . . . that I love her and Tuck with all my heart . . . and I'm going to do my best to make things right."

He had both hands to his forehead and he appeared broken in spirit. There was none of the cocky arrogance left. The reputation he had built and carefully nurtured in the county would be permanently tarnished. His law practice would suffer. But none of that concerned him now. It would be easy to blame the liquor but he knew that would do him no good. He had taken too much for granted for much too long. The divorce papers had an immediate and chilling effect.

"I don't think you need us preaching to you at this point," sighed W. T. "About a half hour ago I was ready to break your face for beating up on my daughter and grandson, but now you know what you need to do. For some strange reason I don't understand myself, I'm gonna bet you are man enough to do it."

"Thanks, W. T."

W. T., Joe Allen, and Carlton walked back to the truck, putting their weapons in the back. John Charles exchanged words with the last few men to leave the VFW hut and drove slowly out of the parking lot.

Before returning home that evening, a vote to disband the Grace Vespers Committee was unanimous. They agreed that vigilante work was not their style. They also vowed to improve their billiards skills and agreed to more fishing trips to Feather Point Lake, all the while keeping an eye on John Charles. W. T.'s son-in-law needed counsel of a different kind now, support from older, more experienced gentlemen who can better understand a man's losses.

Sweet Grass Reunion

Sweet Grass, Georgia
Population: 5,012

"Hi there, Bobby Barham," she gushed. "I'm so happy you came. It's just wonderful to see you again!"

"It's nice to see you, Alice Faye. It's been a long time."

She moved in closer to him, whispering, "I must tell you that I have never stopped thinking about you and the wonderful times we had together in high school."

"That's nice of you to say."

She giggled. "I hope it won't embarrass you for me to admit that I have never stopped loving you."

"Well, I'm flattered, Alice Faye."

She grabbed him by the arm and led him toward the chairs at the end of the gym. "You just have to come over here and sit with me. I must hear every detail about your life since high school."

Alice Faye was acting slightly nervous, almost breathless in her invitation. She still had the ash-blond hair, powder-blue eyes, and a fetching figure. There was a bit more make up than necessary and a little extra waistline; that is, more than he had remembered from two decades ago. Little did he know what this unexpected reunion would bring in the days ahead.

Four months earlier Robert Wilson Barham was sitting at the breakfast table of his modest apartment in Waycross, Georgia, thumbing through the day's mail. There were the usual unsolicited sale magazines, advertisements and utility bills, as well as a note from his aunt Matilda Barham in Sweet Grass. The next item caught his eye—large brown envelope aching to be opened. It was an invitation to a June gathering of the Sweet Grass High School Class of 1953.

He added it to the throwaway pile, then had second thoughts. There had been other reunion invitations, all scheduled in neat five-year intervals. He had not responded to a single one, electing to take a pass on his old high school days. Maybe this time he should reconsider.

Bobby Barham was a better-than-average student, active on the school newspaper—the *Sweet Grass Messenger*—and a forward on the varsity basketball team. There were no compelling reasons to return to Sweet Grass after graduation except an occasional visit with his aunt Matilda. He had returned two or three times a year, all in response to a special call to help his father's younger sister. Matilda Mae Barham was spoken of as the family's spinster aunt. She had lived in the big two-story house at 43 Live Oak Street for more than fifty years, retiring as business manager and bookkeeper at the Sweet Grass Nursing Home.

He remembered Sunday afternoons spent at the big Victorian home and his aunt Matilda's homemade chocolate chip cookies. He enjoyed sitting with her in the porch swing, munching cookies and listening to her stories. These seemed more vivid to him now than memories of his own home and parents.

His mother and father, both heavy cigarette smokers, died of cancer shortly before he graduated from Georgia Southern. The loss left him empty inside and with bad memories of his family life at Sweet Grass. Accepting the fact that he was alone in the world came with considerable difficulty. The expectation that Aunt Matilda would want his help when she could no longer live by herself gave him a vague sense of discomfort. He accepted the fact that when the time came he would do his family duty, but it didn't mean he had to like it.

Matilda sent him newsy notes from time to time, providing reports on certain elder citizens of Sweet Grass, names he no longer recognized. She tried to keep close contact long after he had graduated from both high school and college.

Matilda was the only family member to attend his marriage to Phyllis Ann McCaskall. The ceremony took place in her hometown of Thomasville, Georgia. This was the most athletic trip Matilda had taken in several years, driving to and from Thomasville with her close friend and next-door neighbor Mildred Albertson. Everything seemed ideal for the start of their marriage. Bobby had accepted a position as history teacher and junior high basketball coach at a school in Thomasville, Phyllis' hometown.

Bobby and Phyllis had dated for only seven months before they decided to marry, all this occurring during his senior year in college. She was the eldest daughter of a Thomasville banker. She majored in elementary education but made no attempt to find a teaching position after graduation. They moved to Thomasville and rented an apartment near the school.

His new wife expressed disappointment in having to live in an apartment, clearly expecting to continue the lifestyle provided by her father. The union had not gone well from the start; neither party was particularly committed to a long-term relationship, nor experienced enough to develop a mature partnership. He discovered early on that they had only one thing in common: They both thought she was wonderful.

The divorce came at the end of their first year. It was quick and uncomplicated. There were no children of the marriage and few assets to be concerned about. Bobby returned to a bachelor's life, moving to the nearby town of Waycross and to a new teaching and coaching job at the high school. The obligations of marriage and the independence of bachelorhood were miles apart in his mind. He determined quickly that bachelorhood suited him well.

Busy teaching history and coaching a basketball team contending for stateside honors, he purposely missed all the interim class reunions at Sweet Grass. He elected not to revisit those high school years and the painful memories of the deaths of his parents.

Bobby's family moved to Sweet Grass from nearby Tallahassee, Florida, when he was in the tenth grade. Most of the students in his class had grown up together in the small farming community, knowing each other, as well as members of each other's families from the first grade on. He did well in class work and was a welcomed addition to the basketball team. Beyond that, he always felt like an outsider. He developed only one close friend, a fellow basketball team member named Jake Legrand. He and Jake had double-dated on several occasions, and Jake married his college sweetheart Becky Brothers shortly after graduation. Jake, a business administration major, found a management-training job with a wood products company headquartered in Waycross. The friendship was renewed when Bobby moved to Waycross after the divorce.

Bobby and Jake found time to play an occasional round of weekend golf and take fishing trips out to Wishbone Lake. Jake and Becky had two sons: Brian, age one, and Travis, a three-year-old. The boys instantly adopted him as Uncle Bobby. He tried his best to spoil the little fellows, treating them to ice cream shop visits, taking them to a nearby park, providing an afternoon break for the parents. He even filled in as an occasional babysitter in emergencies.

Alice Faye Gibson had been Bobby's steady girlfriend his senior high school year. She was a member of the cheerleading squad and had personality to spare. She still displayed a hyperactive nature twenty years later, talking in rapid-fire sentences with a high-pitched voice that trailed off in italics. He had enjoyed taking her to movies in Valdosta, the nearest town with a theater. They were also a regular couple at the Friday night sock hops at the school gym. In the small town south in the 1950s it was fashionable to "go steady." So, Bobby and Alice Faye were known as an item. Many of the steady couples were considering marriage shortly after high school. Bobby and Alice Faye had no such plans. In fact, they never discussed marriage or anything beyond high school. Theirs was not a serious relationship as he had just thought of her as a good friend. From time to time he got the impression she might have wanted more, but they moved on to different universities and different lives. He heard that Alice Faye had married a U. S. Air Force officer whose career had taken them all over the globe. Long periods of separation eventually took its toll.

Bobby read the reunion material carefully, trying to picture the names and faces of those listed as members of the Anniversary Steering Committee. He hadn't kept in touch with any classmates or teachers over the past two decades, other than Jake Legrand. Beyond that, Bobby barely remembered the coaches. Something about a two-decade gathering appealed to him. In any case, Aunt Matilda had been trying to persuade him to come to Sweet Grass for a visit. He decided to call Jake to see if he had plans to attend.

I need to go see Aunt Matilda, he thought. *Might as well wound two birds with one stone.*

Bobby Barham felt right at home in the Georgia town, enjoying the atmosphere, the good-old-boy ribbing at the few restaurants in the area. His passion was professional sports and all his travels away from school and coaching involved attending major sports events. He made extra effort to get tickets for the Kentucky Derby, the Super Bowl, and games of the Final Four in college basketball. He put his name in the lottery for tickets to the Masters Golf Tournament in nearby Augusta. He had been saving all year for a trip to London to see Wimbledon for the first time. All his savings went into travel, especially during the summer months and school holidays.

Sweet Grass was a community of just over 5,000, located in the farming country of South Georgia. The locals produced peanuts, cotton, corn and watermelons. There were several peach orchards nearby and almost every family farm had a pecan orchard. The makeshift farmers' market at the edge of town brought customers from nearby towns to shop for fresh produce on the weekends.

Bobby was disappointed to learn that Jake Legrand had to be away on a business trip to Atlanta the weekend of the reunion and could not attend. Still, he filled out the postcard return-reply form to let the committee know that he planned to be there.

Bobby left early in the morning to drive to Sweet Grass, checking in with his aunt Matilda before the reunion events began. She was overjoyed to see him and had the guest bedroom ready. In the late afternoon he drove to the gymnasium. It was just as he had remembered it, small in comparison to one in Waycross where he coached. It was eighty-four feet long by fifty feet wide. Even though it was decorated in crepe paper of the school colors, and a large welcoming sign for the class of 1953, Bobby recognized a distinctive smell. The gym was musty, dank and the air held the scent of sweaty tennis shoes, liniment for sore muscles, and of urinals that had seen much service.

The committee had decorated an elaborate wall of the gym, filling it with photos and posters from 1952–53. There were tables laden with memorabilia, including yearbooks and copies of the school newspaper. A steady flow of music from the era filled that end of the gym. The anniversary committee had a special selection of 45-rpm records and large loudspeakers were stationed at the far end of the building.

Frankie Lane sang "High Noon." There was Bill Haley and His Comets with "Crazy, Man, Crazy," and the fifties atmosphere returned with a steady stream of hits from The Four Aces, Perry Como, Patti Page and Eddie Fisher.

After introductions by the Class President Marvin Adkins, now owner of the only decent restaurant in Sweet Grass, there were recognitions of those traveling the farthest to attend, those with the most children, those who were married the shortest and longest, and an embarrassing review of those voted the traditional series of "Most Likely to's."

The reception conversation was loud and Bobby suspected the punch bowl had been laced with an adult beverage. There was a slightly different taste that he couldn't recognize. The buffet dinner—garden salad, pork tenderloin, roasted potatoes, and green beans—was a big hit and dancing was encouraged afterwards. He was headed for the dessert table and some lemon icebox pie when the music of Jonnie Ray filled the gym with his hit record "Walking My Baby Back Home." Alice Faye reappeared at Bobby's side, insisting that they dance.

They joined other couples on the gym floor, and she snuggled close under his chin, holding on tighter than he had expected. The steps came back to him and he moved her around with ease. The record came to an end and she balked as he tried to return her to a seat.

"I just dearly love this," she said. "I honestly prayed that you would be here this year. Let's wait for the next song."

The familiar musical intro to Teresa Brewer's hit record "Til I Waltz Again With You" followed and Alice Faye was even more accommodating this time around, cuddling on his shoulder in a way that drew the attention of others on the dance floor. Willis Reader, a former guard on the basketball team, danced by with his wife Marcie and he winked at Bobby with an attaboy grin. Bobby tried to act with casual indifference, but was clearly uncomfortable with her aggressive style. Finally, he persuaded her to take a break and escorted her to the punch bowl.

"This brings back such wonderful memories," she said, looking up at him with a longing that ached in her eyes. "I have missed you soooo much all these years. Have you ever thought of me? Have you missed me, too?"

"We had a very good friendship, Alice Faye," he said, glancing over his shoulder to see if anyone was close enough to overhear her sentiments. "It was a nice high school thing we had and I do remember you fondly as my first real sweetheart."

He tried to choose his words carefully, attempting to strike a balance between not offending or embarrassing her and encouraging nothing further. She had a puzzled reaction, a slight frown on her forehead, quickly followed by a large smile an invitation for him to accompany her to talk with a group gathered near the record player. She elected to ignore his tactful, albeit noncommittal, response.

"Remember my old high school boyfriend?" she announced to the group. "Isn't he just as handsome as ever?"

He tried several times to move away from Alice Faye and visit with others, especially members of the basketball team. She seemed always to be stationed near his left elbow.

The evening and the reunion activities closed with a solemn memorial to those classmates who had died. The names were read aloud as soft music played in the background. At the conclusion Marvin Adkins reminded all of the next get-together in five years. He encouraged them to make plans far in advance to assure attendance. A committee would soon be formed to begin plans for a special twenty-fifth Sweet Grass reunion for the class of 1953. He made an open invitation for committee volunteers.

Aunt Matilda was waiting for Bobby when he returned to the big white-framed house on Live Oak Street, anxious to hear a full report on all the evening's activities. She had coffee on and had made a pound cake, remembering that it was one of his favorites.

Bobby loosened his tie, slipped off his shoes and poured a cup for himself and his aunt. He accompanied her to the parlor and sat in a large wingback chair. The Victorian home had a distinctive smell, the musty tell-tell sign of aging. Aunt Matilda, her night robe pulled tight at her neck, wanted to know everything and the questions came in a rush. He accommodated her by describing the decorations, the reunion program, the meal and several school chums from twenty years before, the few he had a chance to talk with for any length of time. She hung on his every word and had more pointed questions about specific names, several now-grown children of her church friends and co-workers at the nursing home.

He found himself relaxing in a way he hadn't all day, enjoying her reactions to his recounting of certain events. He even embellished a tale or two just for her benefit.

"What was the most special part of the reunion?" she asked.

"You won't believe it, Aunt Matilda," he whispered, leaning forward for dramatic effect. "Some of the homeliest girls in my graduating class turned out to be damn good-looking women!"

Aunt Matilda howled with delight.

They nibbled on cake, sipped coffee and talked well past the dinner hour. He was tired and eager to get some rest, but his aunt was so pleased with his visit and the special attention he gave her, that the conversation continued until midnight. Bobby was careful to make no mention of his old girlfriend Alice Faye Gibson. He was relieved that his aunt had not asked about her.

Aunt Matilda persuaded him to stay one more day, letting her take him on a tour of the town and surrounding area. She wanted to show him the new buildings and businesses established since his last visit, as well as the new county park just west of Sweet Grass. Her real reason was to show him off to several of her bridge partners and friends from the ladies' auxiliary at the Grace Methodist Church. He promised he would stay only if she would let him treat her to dinner the next evening at Marvin Adkin's restaurant, The Sweet Grass Grill.

Both Matilda and Bobby slept late the following morning. He was finally roused out of bed by the smell of coffee. Matilda had pancakes and bacon waiting for him when he wandered into the kitchen in his pajamas. The phone rang before he had poured the first cup.

Matilda answered the call, handing him the phone. "It's for you, Bobby."

He put the receiver to his ear and flinched at the enthusiastic greeting from Alice Faye Gibson.

"I hope you had a wonderful night's rest," she said. "I just wanted to tell you what a beautiful evening it was for me, and how much I enjoyed dancing with you. This weekend has brought back such terrific memories for me that I just can't let it stop here."

"It was nice seeing you again, Alice Faye, and I'm glad you had such a good time."

"I was wondering if we couldn't have dinner together tonight before you leave for home?"

"Really, Alice Faye, I must tell you that I already have a date with my aunt Matilda this evening."

"That's just wonderful," she said. "I would love to meet your aunt. Please bring her along. We could go over to Valdosta, just like old times!"

"Alice Faye, please don't consider me rude or unkind, but this was a long standing visit with my aunt and she and I have some family business to attend to. Sorry, but I just can't go to Valdosta with you tonight."

There was a silent moment on the other end of the line as Alice Faye collected her thoughts and reorganized a plan of attack.

"Well, I do understand, but you will have to promise me that we can get together for a long afternoon and late dinner sometime very soon."

"Sure," he sighed. "We'll just have to do that sometime."

They exchanged closing pleasantries and his facial expression told Aunt Matilda much of the story.

"Was that Alice Faye Gibson?" she asked.

"Yes it was, and she has much stronger memories of our high school romance than I do."

He told her about the activities of the past evening, including Alice Faye's insistence that he stay at her side. He gave details about their long stretches on the dance floor with her unusual demonstrations of affection.

Aunt Matilda filled in some gossip about Alice Faye's marriage to the Air Force officer, things she had heard at the Rachel Campbell's beauty shop. "Reba Montgomery, Alice Faye's aunt, told me the divorce was very unpleasant. I don't remember exactly what the problem was. I think he may have had other girlfriends during his travels. Anyway, I don't like to listen to stuff like that."

The conversation changed to questions about his future plans. Aunt Matilda was concerned about what would happen to her as she aged, understanding that she would not be able to care for herself alone much longer in such a big house.

Bobby promised to make certain she was okay, assuring her that he would come to her aid if anything happened.

"You're going to outlive all of us," he kidded. "I may have to count on you to take care of me, especially if I have more troubles with Alice Faye Gibson."

Back home in Waycross, Bobby sat down with the calendar to determine just how many weeks of summer he had left before the next school year. He was trying to decide if he had time to take one more trip to the Midwest for some professional baseball before the division playoffs. His thoughts included a Cleveland Indian's game, Chicago and a White Sox outing, down to St. Louis and a visit to Busch Stadium, then on to Little Rock for a Minor League contest between the Arkansas Travelers and maybe the Memphis Chicks or Shreveport Sports.

He called Jake Legrand that evening, inviting him to lunch the next day at the Waycross Grill on the town square. He promised to fill Jake in on all the details of the reunion he had missed.

At a table near the front, one occupied often by the pair, Bobby and Jake sipped sweet tea and tried to catch up on the events of the past week. Jake's trip to Atlanta had been uneventful and he was more than disappointed at having missed the gathering of his class in Sweet Grass.

"Do you remember Alice Faye Gibson?" Bobby asked.

"Sure, she was one of the real good-lookers! In fact, didn't you two go steady during our senior year?

"True enough."

"I remember that we double-dated several times. Remember that night we took them to the drive in over in Valdosta? Boy, that was a hoot! I remember you and Alice Faye were in the back seat and things got real steamy!"

"That's enough, I don't need to hear about that. . . . She was at the reunion!"

"Really, is she still a looker?

"Not only was she there, Jake, she latched on to me during the cocktail hour and I couldn't get away from her all evening. She was all over me like a rash. It got to be embarrassing."

"I heard she is now divorced. Hey, she's in the same fix as you, Bobby. Maybe this is the big romantic opportunity you've been waiting for."

"Not funny, Jake!"

Jake then got a full report on her behavior, including her dominating his evening. He expressed discomfort in her insistence that they stay on the dance floor, and how she had confessed special affection for him, lasting from twenty years before. He told Jake about her telephone call the next morning at his aunt's house.

Jake didn't have much to offer in the way of support. He expressed sympathy and suggested that Bobby tell her he was engaged or maybe had homosexual tendencies.

"Still not funny, Jake!"

The second week back home brought a perfumed letter in a decorative envelope; the return address was in Atlanta and the scent was all too familiar.

My dearest Bobby,

I wanted to pen this quick note to again thank you for spending so much time with me during the beautiful weekend at Sweet Grass. It was such a treat to see you and to renew our friendship. You have been an important part of my memories over these past decades as someone very special to me. As I told you at the reunion, I never really stopped loving you. I could tell that you continued to have good feelings about me and of the times we spent together. Now that we have been reunited, I don't ever want to lose that again.

I want to invite you to visit me in Atlanta very soon. I have a nice apartment in the Buckhead area and you can fulfill your promise to take me to dinner. You could even count on much more. Call me and let me know what weekend you will be available. I understand it is only about a five-hour drive.

Do call soon and let me know when you can come. I haven't looked forward to anything so much in years. My heart will just ache until I hear from you!

With all my love,

Alice Faye

Bobby sat and stared at the letter, wondering just how he had gotten himself into this predicament. He read it a second time, trying to think of anything especially inviting he might have said or done during the first meeting with her at the reunion. He was certain their time together twenty years ago was based solely on teenage friendship, certainly not to the level of a serious courtship or love affair. He found the whole thing puzzling.

The next two weeks went by slowly. He had no intention of calling Alice Faye Gibson, and he certainly would not be spending a weekend with her in the Atlanta apartment. Just thinking about it all brought back bad memories of his married days. The yearlong experience with Phyllis had been the most trying of his life. It was a particular pain he did not want to revisit.

Bobby was admittedly gun-shy about committing to another serious relationship. Besides, he could travel to any sports event anytime he didn't have to work, and was not accountable to anyone. There were times when he thought about female companionship and having children of his own. He imagined teaching a little son how to fish, kick a soccer ball with both feet, how to tag up on a fly ball, and how to balance yourself for a set shot just outside the free throw line. Maybe someday he would find just the right lady. He didn't consider thirty-seven too old to have children. Maybe he would be ready for another try one day, but not right away. He could find no reason to rush the process.

There were occasional dates over the past few years, mostly platonic times with single teachers from his school, the ones who needed an escort to a faculty dinner or school events. These were attractive young women who would all eventually find steady men friends and get married. He was always invited to their weddings. He was considered just a very nice guy, the unattached coach who was available, pleasant company, and harmless.

The telephone rang just as he stepped through the door to his apartment, returning from a workout at the gym. He dropped his gym bag on the floor and reached for the receiver.

"Yes, this is Bobby Barham."

"Hi, Bobby . . . this is Alice Faye, and I have some absolutely wonderful news for you!"

"Really," he said. "What's that?"

"I am coming to Thomasville weekend after next for a meeting at the Rockledge Inn, a regional fund-raising seminar for nonprofit organizations. Isn't that just great?"

"I think you will enjoy the trip."

"Truth is," she said, "I am really just a volunteer at the Arts Council of Atlanta and help sometimes with special events. I don't really have to attend all the sessions if I don't want to. So, after I register and get credit for being there, I would love to come over to Waycross and see you. You could show me the town and we could have that special dinner you promised."

His mind raced. What was he going to do now? The trip to Chicago and beyond became an instant reality.

"I'm so sorry, Alice Faye," he tried to add a tone of disappointment. "I am leaving next Friday for a trip to Chicago and several cities in the Midwest. I'll be gone for almost three weeks."

"Oh no!" There was pain in her voice.

"Jake Legrand from our class lives here with his wife Becky. I know you remember them? We double-dated a few times. They have two kids that are just adorable. I'll tell him you are coming and I'm certain Jake or Becky could show you around."

"I really wanted you to give me the tour, Bobby. I was looking forward to our spending more time together."

"It just can't be helped, Alice Faye. I will have to leave this coming weekend."

"I am so, so disappointed."

The conversation lasted a short time more, ending with strained and awkward good-byes. In the process she had exacted another promise to spend some time with her in Atlanta. She outlined in unusual detail her plans for their dinner, describing the menu and restaurant she had chosen especially for the occasion. She noted that there was plenty of room for him to stay in her apartment and there were hints at what could be in store later in the evening.

Bobby hung up the receiver and realized that his nerves were now on edge. He went to the kitchen in search of a cold beer. The tension in his back and shoulders was intense. This was far too much. Why had he gone to that reunion? He had no interest in renewing a relationship with Alice Faye Gibson. This long ago high school friend and companion had gone from casual acquaintance to a genuine annoyance. The whole dinner obsession and plans for an evening in her Atlanta apartment sounded like a well-constructed trap.

The following morning he began packing a bag for the driving trip to the Midwest. His initial enthusiasm for attending several baseball games in Cleveland, Chicago, St. Louis, and Memphis was dampened now, conditioned by the forced change of schedule to escape Alice Faye Gibson. He didn't like the feeling, sensations that brought back the agony of those difficult months with his former wife. He called Jake to tell him he was leaving the following morning, to warn him of a possible call from Alice Faye, and to let him know when he would return.

Before the coffeepot began to perc the next morning, Bobby's telephone rang. His first instinct was not to answer it. He let it ring two times more than usual before picking up the receiver, holding his breath and hoping it would not be Alice Faye.

"Good morning, Bobby," a voice he did not immediately recognize. "This is Mildred Albertson, your aunt Matilda's next door neighbor in Sweet Grass."

"Certainly, Mildred," he was relieved. "You and Aunt Matilda came to my wedding, and I saw you last time I was in Sweet Grass. Do you and my aunt still play canasta?"

"We did, Bobby." Her tone was somber. "I have some very bad news to report. Your aunt Matilda died in her sleep last night."

"Oh no! It can't be. She was doing just fine last month."

"They believe it was her heart, Bobby." Mildred's voice begins to break and she fought back tears, saying, "I just thank the Lord she didn't have to suffer."

They talked about plans for a funeral and the need for him to return to Sweet Grass to help attend to things. He thanked her for the call and her friendship with his aunt, promising he would leave right away for Sweet Grass. He explained his travel plans for the Midwest and that he was already packed. The baseball adventure would now be postponed indefinitely.

He dialed Jake Legrand's number as soon as he hung up from Mildred's call, reporting the death of his aunt and another change of plans. Jake offered genuine sympathy and asked if there was anything he and Becky could do. Bobby allowed as how he would have much to do with arrangements for the funeral and decisions to be made about his aunt's home and belongings. He speculated that he may be away as long as two weeks.

Neighbors and friends gathered at the big house on Live Oak Street, bringing along sympathy and casseroles. Miss Matilda, as she was known in Sweet Grass, was a popular citizen of the little town. People came to offer assistance: staff members from the nursing home as well as fellow members of her ladies' auxiliary and Sunday school class at the Methodist church. That's what people in the small-town South do. They gather at the death of any neighbor or friend, supporting the family and showering them with an abundance of comfort food. This would be the case in the death of any well-known citizen of Sweet Grass.

Bobby drove to Sweet Grass, arriving in time to visit with the Reverend Wallace Delony, pastor of the Grace Methodist Church. Reverend Delony made recommendations concerning the day and time for the funeral, to be held in the sanctuary. Mildred Albertson was ever present, helping with the food and introducing him to all the friends and co-workers gathered at Aunt Matilda's house.

His next stop was at the Chadwick Funeral Home where his aunt's body was being attended to. He met with Fred Chadwick to discuss arrangements, and made the necessary decisions involving services and costs.

He was mentally and physically exhausted when he got back to his aunt's house, hoping the well-meaning and caring people had gone home by then. Many had, but close neighbors and friends remained to visit. To his utter astonishment, there sat Alice Faye Gibson on the living room couch, talking with Mildred Albertson.

She saw him come through the front door and stood to greet him.

"I learned from Jake Legrand that your aunt had died and I just came to be of any assistance I could."

He mumbled something and walked on to the kitchen. Alice Faye and Mildred sat back down and continued their conversation. The coffee was hot and the dining room table piled high with food. A side table held an assortment of pies and cakes. He poured a cup of coffee and returned to the living room, annoyed at the sight of Alice Faye and thoroughly confused as to how to deal with the situation. He had several thoughts in mind of just what to say. However, he entered the living room to find that Alice Faye Gibson was gone.

Mildred asked if there was anything more she could do to help. If not, she needed to go next door and feed her cats.

"Thank you for everything, Mildred," he said. "I don't know how we could have gotten through all this without you. The funeral will be at 10:00 A.M. tomorrow, and I would like very much for you to sit with me down front."

She accepted his invitation and started for the door.

"By the way, Mildred, where did Alice Faye Gibson go?"

"What a nice young women," she said. "She and I had a very interesting conversation and you are lucky to have such a friend."

"But where did she go?"

"She is staying at the Carriage House Motel over on Wiseman Street, the one right at the intersection to the Valdosta highway. She thought you would be tired and didn't want to be a bother."

The house grew silent. Streetlights on Live Oak came on. It seemed eerie to be in this house without his aunt. For the first time since learning of her death, he sat down in the favorite armchair, the one he had occupied so often during visits with his aunt. His parents were gone and now so was Aunt Matilda. He experienced for the first time an emptiness he didn't know how to fill. He slumped back and felt big salty tears running down his cheeks. He sat there for a long time, trying to come to grips with a series of questions about his life, questions he had managed to avoid for decades. They all came at him now, surfacing all at one time. Did he really want to coach and teach all the way to retirement? Was he using his talent to the best end? Could he be missing something more interesting and exciting? Did he really want to live alone? Would things be much more fulfilling if there was a loving woman in his life? Finally, he retired to the back bedroom but sleep didn't come for a time.

The following morning he woke to heavy cloud cover and steady drizzle. Why did it rain every time there was a funeral? He couldn't remember ever attending one or even seeing a funeral procession without rain? *God must be crying,* he thought. The sanctuary of the First Methodist Church was packed a half hour before the service was to begin. Alice Faye Gibson sat in the back, dressed in a plain black dress with pearl earrings and a black scarf covering her hair. Bobby saw her as he and Mildred passed by on their way to the front pew. Alice Faye had done something different with her hair and she seemed more attractive than he had remembered.

Reverend Delony conducted the service with kind words and thoughts appropriate to the deceased and the occasion. Aunt Matilda was buried next to his parents in the Sweet Grass Cemetery. Most of those attending the funeral followed on to the cemetery with a colorful assortment of umbrellas. And then it was all over. Aunt Matilda was no more and Bobby faced a new set of decisions: how to handle the disposition of her estate, what to do with his aunt's belongings, and what about the house. For some strange reason his aunt's death had affected him in a much more profound way than expected.

Back on Live Oak Street, dozens of Aunt Matilda's friends gathered to reminisce and offer condolences, another of the customs of Sweet Grass. He escaped to the back bedroom and changed from suit and tie to a more comfortable polo shirt and slacks.

As he returned through the kitchen he spied Alice Faye, also in a change of outfits. She was in the process of moving food from the refrigerator back to the dining room table, arranging the cakes and pies as before. She had made fresh coffee; placed napkins and paper plates out for the guests and proceeded to help the older women who had made camp in the living room. He stood silently watching her, amazed at her proficiency.

Alice Faye seemed far too busy to notice him or acknowledge his presence. She moved with ease among the ladies, asking their names, making small talk, seeking their comfort and constantly refilling coffee cups and juice glasses.

He talked with the well-wishers, listening to their many tales about his aunt, hearing over and over again what a wonderful person she was and how profoundly she would be missed. All the while, Mildred and Alice Faye had taken charge and were handling everything. From the corner of his eye, Bobby was fascinated at the smooth working relationship between the two women, something he did not expect from Alice Faye Gibson.

People drifted away as the afternoon moved along. Mildred and Alice Faye put away the food, tidied up the living and dining rooms and cleaned the kitchen counters. As dusk approached, Bobby saw the last of the visitors to the door. Mildred also said her good-byes with the admonition for him to keep in touch and let her know what she could do to help in any way about the house and Matilda's belongings. Alice Fay was close behind Mildred, retrieving her handbag and telling him again how sorry she was about his loss.

"Where are you going, Alice Faye?"

"Back to the motel. I know you need to get some rest."

"Tell me again how you even knew about Aunt Matilda's death?"

"I had called Jake Legrand to let him know I would not be coming to Thomasville and he told me all about it, about your aunt's death and that you would not be going on your sports trip."

"You didn't need to come all the way down here, but it was very nice of you. And I really appreciate all the help you were over the last couple of days. You and Mildred were lifesavers. I wouldn't have known what to do."

"Jake is a very good friend to you," she said, "and he also has the guts to tell a person like me the truth I needed to hear."

They were standing in the living room and she was angling toward the front door, still intending to make a quiet exit.

"What truth?" he asked.

"Jake told me what a nuisance I had made of myself at the reunion and afterwards, and how you had reacted negatively to my behavior. I realize now that I have been making a fool of myself, that I came on too strong. I am very sorry about how I've been acting and I'm truly ashamed of myself."

"You don't need to be that hard on yourself."

"I came here to attend the funeral, to support you if I could, to apologize for the way I have been acting and to let you know that it will not happen again."

"I don't know what to say, Alice Faye."

"Just say you forgive me and I won't bother you anymore." She inched closer to the door, saying, "I'll head back for Atlanta first thing in the morning."

This all took Bobby by surprise. So much had happened in the past few days. Her change of demeanor was confusing and disarming, but also refreshing.

"Alice Faye, how would you like to drive over to Valdosta with me tonight for dinner?"

"You must be kidding with all those leftovers in the refrigerator."

"Well, we can have dinner right here then. I actually prefer leftovers."

She wanted desperately to say "yes" and spend the night with him, but her new view of the universe, prompted by their schoolmate Jake, told her it was not the right thing to do.

"Alice Faye, please sit down, I believe we have more to talk about."

The atmosphere changed. He couldn't believe how different she was from the schoolgirl infatuation displayed at the reunion. She came across now as a mature, thoughtful woman with much to give and no one to give it too. They opened a bottle of wine. They reminisced about old times in Sweet Grass. They talked about the years afterwards and shared information about the painful divorces each had suffered. She confessed an emotional drifting in recent months and a loneliness that left her feeling useless. She wanted to find a new job where she was engaged in doing something worthwhile and where she could rekindle her energy and enthusiasm. She finally realized that she could do that with or without a man in her life.

He talked about his dreams and aspirations, expressing a waning interest in teaching and coaching. He had another confession: He had resisted the urge to reconnect with her because he could not chance another failed relationship. Since the painful divorce he had carefully developed defense mechanisms to protect himself from emotional involvement with other women and the potential for more harm. He had been afraid to let Alice Faye back in his life.

They talked well past midnight, forgetting about food. He asked her to stay for the night, and she declined. She would return to the motel, but would do so with a restored feeling of self-esteem and a happy heart, a satisfaction she had not experienced for quite some time. Even if she no longer needed a relationship with her old sweetheart, it was the most healing conversation she had experienced in years. Someone she cared about had actually listened to her, valued her points of view, and offered sympathy as well as encouragement.

Bobby saw her to the car. He surprised himself by reaching for her shoulders, turning her toward him, taking her in his arms and kissing her good-bye. It was a long, deeply satisfying kiss. The sensation almost took them both back to 1953.

Alice Faye pulled out of the driveway, looking back to wave goodbye. She left for Atlanta the next morning with no plan to see Bobby Barham ever again.

To Believe in Angels

Skidaway Island, Georgia
Population: 6,767

He arrived at half-past five, following his usual schedule for an evening meal at the Plantation Club. A young waitress greeted him as he entered the main dining room.

"Good evening, sir. Here for dinner?" she asked with unusual enthusiasm.

"Yes, thank you." He detected a slight nervousness in her voice, a waitress he had not seen before.

The first diner to arrive, he headed straight for his regular seat at a window table overlooking a lagoon and the eighteenth green of the Palmetto Golf Course.

"Could I take your drink order, or should we wait for your wife?"

"My wife won't be coming," he said.

"Oh, I am sorry," she said, "I thought she might have stopped at the ladies' room."

"No, actually, my wife died of cancer about nine months ago."

"I am so embarrassed," she said obviously shaken. "This is my first week here and I didn't know."

"Its quite all right," he offered quickly. "No need to be embarrassed. I thought you might be a new employee. . . . Didn't think I'd seen you here before."

"I am so very sorry," she continued.

"Why don't you just bring me an attitude adjustment," he said. "Make that a bourbon Manhattan on the rocks." He made the request as much an effort to ease the awkward moment as to satisfy his thirst.

That was how George R. Wardlaw met the new Plantation waitress LaKisha Marie Barber. It was a rather messy beginning, but a beginning nonetheless. Most of the dinner crowd at The Landings, a gated golf and boating community near Savannah, Georgia, didn't arrive until 6:00 P.M. or later. George and his wife Mary Margaret had been early regulars most weekday evenings. They occasionally patronized the other three clubhouses, but Plantation was nearest their home and a favorite.

In 1989, George sold Wardlaw Printing Company to a competitor at a handsome profit and persuaded Mary Margaret to leave the suburbs of Philadelphia in search of salt air and sunshine. At age sixty-nine he was ready for retirement and a slower pace, a welcomed break after more than forty years of the long hours it took to build a successful printing business.

They made several trips from Charleston down the Eastern Seaboard to Florida, searching for the perfect retirement spot. Entirely by accident they chanced upon Skidaway, one of the Georgia barrier islands located just southeast of Savannah. On their second trip to Skidaway, home of The Landings community, they bought a patio home on the south end of the island. It was the best move of their lives and led to the most satisfying decade of a forty-seven-year marriage. It just ended too soon.

George was supposed to die first. That was his plan. He understood the mortality tables and the fact that women in the United States live an average of five to seven years longer than men. He and Mary Margaret knew a number of widow ladies at The Landings and expected one day she would join them. He made certain she knew how he had managed their assets and how their retirement income was arranged. He showed her several times where to find all the tax records and insurance policies. She pretended to be interested just to appease George. None of that mattered anymore, he was alone and he missed her more than mere words could explain. Their union had been of the old-fashioned type, where marriage vows were for real and forever.

When the waitress brought the drink, George asked her name and how she had come to work at The Landings. LaKisha Barber was the single parent of a two-year-old daughter, and worked two jobs to keep things together as best she could. While George nursed his bourbon and LaKisha waited for more diners, they talked.

LaKisha grew up in the city of Savannah and had graduated from Jenkins High School two years before. Her boyfriend, the father of her daughter, told her he loved her and wanted to get married. That was before he learned about her pregnancy. With that news he simply disappeared. His friends didn't know what happened to him, and she had not heard a word from him since. Her mother took care of the child while LaKisha worked as a cashier at Kroger's during the day. She applied for and got The Landings waitress job in the evenings as a way to bring in more income.

George finished reading the *Savannah Morning News* and poured the remains of a second cup of coffee down the drain. He changed into walking shoes and left by way of the garage door. He covered two miles every morning, the same tract he and Mary Margaret had walked several mornings each week. For the past nine months, George had been making the morning walk alone.

He went out to Landings Way South, following the street to a bike and jogging path that paralleled Delegal Creek. This had been Mary Margaret's favorite part of the walk. There was the usual morning breeze off Ossabaw Sound. Squirrels scurried across the path and jumped to the sides of nearby trees, sneaking a peek from the far side to watch him pass. At certain times of the year, black feral hogs appeared across Delegal Creek on the eastern side of uninhabited Green Island. Marsh rabbits came out to nibble new grasses along the path in the springtime. George and Mary Margaret loved the island atmosphere and told friends back in Philadelphia that they lived in a national park, or so it seemed.

Cancer is a terrible thing, affecting the mind as well as the body. Neither George nor Mary Margaret had experienced serious medical problems during their marriage, enjoying unusually healthy lives; that is, other than the sad fact that Mary Margaret had been unable to have children. At one point they discussed adoption, but eventually abandoned the idea. Mary Margaret began complaining of unusual headaches the year before. She tired easily and felt nauseated several times during the day. A trip to the family doctor at SouthCoast Medical produced no real answers. Her doctor insisted she see a specialist, and made all the arrangements.

After a number of trips to specialists in Jacksonville, Florida, the problem was diagnosed as a glioma tumor, a particularly damaging type that tends to sprout quickly and spread throughout the brain. Brain tumors have always been one of the most difficult diseases to treat, much less to cure. Approximately 20,000 Americans contract the disease annually, with more than half of them dying within eighteen months. Mary Margaret suffered through a series of treatments, but died within the year. George suffered with her in his own way, and it took its toll, especially on his spirit.

George stopped on a footbridge crossing a large lagoon near the Delegal Marina. He listened to the sounds of the morning, thinking that the early walks would never be the same. He heard a marsh hen calling her mate. A flock of ibis, white-winged creatures with hooked beaks, flew out of the wax myrtle trees beside the lagoon, circling over the water and heading south to begin the day's search for food. This particular bridge was a favorite spot offering another reason to stop and observe the wildlife. A large set of eyes in deep sockets moved slowly through the water with its broad snout just above the surface. On this day an alligator appeared near the bank on the east side of the bridge. He and Mary Margaret had seen this same alligator often, and she had even given it the pet name Allie. An occasional mullet jumped from the surface of the water, returning with a splash to feed on algae and other marine matter. He wondered just how long he could continue the morning walks.

Within a week, when George arrived at the Plantation Club, LaKisha had his favorite chair pulled back, the napkin unfolded and a bourbon Manhattan waiting at his place. She always had a big grin on her face as he took his seat. Over the next several weeks their brief conversations became a welcomed ritual. LaKisha made certain his bourbon was waiting at the right time and they had a few minutes to visit each evening before the larger dinner crowd arrived.

"You are hands down the very best waitress at The Landings," he kidded her, and she loved his special attention. He asked a lot of questions, and she was comfortable telling him about her life. She confessed that her ambition was to one day go to college and get a degree in nursing. Her favorite courses in high school were in science and she was convinced that nursing would be a great fit. That's why she was working two jobs, raising a daughter, getting little sleep, trying to save enough for college tuition.

George answered LaKisha's questions about where and how he had met a pretty Irish girl named Mary Margaret Kelley. It was during their junior year at Seton Hall University in East Orange, New Jersey. He majored in business, she in English. A friend at a pep rally for the basketball team introduced them. He wasn't sure any girl had ever smiled at him that way. That night and the next day he couldn't get that smile out of his mind. He called her and invited her for coffee and a movie. They were married during his senior year.

He told LaKisha about his career in the printing business, and how he had borrowed money to buy his first press and open a shop. He talked about the fourteen-hour days he spent making the business grow to the point where he had a 20,000-square-foot building with two large web presses, and the ability to bid for and win major corporate annual report contracts and four-color national magazine projects.

Mary Margaret earned a teacher's certificate and taught English in a middle school. She also taught a special cooking class in an after-school continuing education program for adults, and her specialty was desserts.

LaKisha liked to talk about her daughter, the precocious child she had named Lisa Ann. She had great hopes and aspirations for her, but few of the financial resources to make big dreams come true. Her mother helped as much as she could, and always encouraged LaKisha.

"My mother tells me the harder I work the luckier I'll get," she said. "She promises me that if I treat people right and pay attention to my own business, good things will happen for me and Lisa."

"Your mother is a wise lady," he told her. "I'll bet good things will happen for you."

LaKisha gave a big sigh and smiled. "My momma is always telling me that I just gotta believe in angels."

LaKisha never knew her father. He died when she was an infant. Her mother remained a widow, living now on Social Security. She was also known as the philosopher of the family. Her personally crafted wisdoms were repeated in the neighborhood. "If you are reaching for the rainbow," she told LaKisha, "you also gotta put up with a little rain now and again."

"Do you believe in angels?" George asked her.

"I do," she answered. "I believe in angels for Lisa's sake!"

Prompted by the newcomers' organization at The Landings, George and Mary Margaret joined a bridge club and played with other couples in their homes on Thursday evenings. George played golf on Wednesdays and Fridays with the same group of fellows, enjoying the atmosphere and exercise even though they were never very accomplished at the sport. All the members of his golfing gang had handicaps in the high twenties. A morning round and the bragging-rights wager could result in winning as much as three bucks, or losing the same. They were members of a dining group with wives sharing recipes and making elaborate plans for cocktails and an evening potluck at a member's home. Mary Margaret loved to experiment with new recipes and was most often called upon to provide dessert. Her desserts made her rather famous on the island, including a variety of personally designed trifles, a Polish knedle, tiramisu to die for, and zabaglione, a specialty. She fashioned some extraordinary dishes for fund-raisers that always sold in record time.

George stood on the lagoon bridge for a long time on one of his morning walks, thinking about what an emotional roller coaster ride he was experiencing. Some days he could put the hurt aside and function reasonably well. There were others when he had trouble getting the cobwebs out of his head. There actually is a fate worse than death he thought: not just loneliness, but something deeper that borders on hopelessness. There were nights when he couldn't sleep, battling a feeling of emptiness. George hadn't realized exactly how much Mary Margaret meant to him, how important she was to his sense of well-being. There was just so much he had taken for granted.

His friends—actually their friends—continued to invite him to dinner parties, to movies and on day trips to Charleston or Hilton Head. They were couples; he was just George. An important part of him was missing. It seemed so strange now, since for more than four decades he had been a part of a team, always referred to as George and Mary Margaret. She had been the social member of their union, the partner who never met a stranger. She was the one who easily made conversation with anyone. He relied on her to carry that part of the bargain at cocktail receptions, first-time gourmet dinners and bridge parties. When he accepted invitations now to go out with friends, conversation seemed awkward. The talk often revolved around what they did as couples. He didn't find much to contribute, so he manufactured a series of handy excuses to decline as many invitations as possible. He would have to reorder his life, rethink how to behave and how to interact with other people. He would need to come to grips with the fact that he was very much alone after a close lifelong partnership.

George arrived at the Plantation Club to discover that his cocktail was missing. LaKisha was not there. He asked about her but the other waitresses didn't know for certain why she was away. She had not mentioned time off or a vacation. When she was absent for the third night in a row he looked for the evening manager to inquire about her.

"She called in and asked for some time off," the manager told him. "Actually, I believe it had something to do with transportation, something about her car."

The manager talked about how difficult it was to hire and keep reliable staff for the dining room, and how she would be as accommodating as possible for a good and responsible waitress like LaKisha. George told her how much he enjoyed seeing LaKisha each evening and talking with her. He even put in a few good words about her work performance.

He told himself there was no reason for him to be concerned with LaKish's problems. After all, he was getting to be an old man; retired, a widower, and he had his own issues. It surely would not be appropriate for an island homeowner and club member to be inquiring about a staff employee. Even so, he worried about LaKisha and her daughter. He even tried without success to find a name and number in the Savannah phone book. He knew she lived with her mother on the east side of the city, but not exactly where.

The next morning his golf group had a 9:22 A.M. tee time at the Deer Creek course. He made certain his golf cart had a full charge before heading toward the other side of the island. After the usual amount of kibitzing on the first tee, the game was set and they were off. George made a bogie on the first hole and doubled the second. By the time his foursome reached the fifth tee he had completely lost concentration and could find little interest in the game. His mind kept wandering as he worried about LaKisha and searched for a way to help her with appropriate discretion. That same evening she reappeared at the Plantation Club, his bourbon waiting at the same table.

"What happened to you?" he asked. "I heard you had car troubles."

"My car just died," she said. "Something was wrong with the starter, or something like that. I didn't have the money to get it fixed right away."

"Tell me about your car," he said. "I'm interested in cars."

"I bought it used," she shrugged. "It's a 1989 Chevy, and it also needs new tires."

Her cousin had been persuaded to drive her to work for a few evenings and a fellow waitress promised to take her home at the end of their shift. "I couldn't miss work any more," she told him. "We have rent due next week."

They talked more about how and where to have her car repaired and she was very interested in his recommendations. As soon as she delivered his salad and crab cakes, four couples arrived with a single reservation. LaKisha scurried over to direct them to a special table set up for them. The group had just come from a reception and immediately ordered another round of drinks. They were loud and obviously enjoying each other's company. LaKisha moved around the table, taking orders. She occasionally glanced over her shoulder at George and smiled, making certain he was taken care of.

The next evening George arrived on time, greeted LaKisha, thanked her for his bourbon and handed her an envelope.

"What is this for?" she asked with a puzzled look.

"Just thought you could use a hand."

LaKisha opened the envelope and found a set of car keys. George explained that his wife's car, a Buick sedan, had been in their garage unused since her death and he hadn't yet decided what to do with it. He described the car as light green in color and assured her it had a full tank of gas. He told here just where it was parked near the ballroom entrance. "Just drive it until you can get yours repaired," he said.

"I can't do that," she frowned. "I can't take your car."

She did take the car and used it for more than two weeks. Somehow she gathered the funds to get her car equipped with a new starter, and was back on the road.

When George and Mary Margaret moved to The Landings, he

considered buying a boat. The idea of spending time on the water and fishing in the sound had a certain appeal. After committing to three golf days per week, plus occasional play in a club-sponsored event on Saturdays, participating in a bridge club and two gourmet dinner groups, he could not imagine when he would have time for boating. He and Mary Margaret also traveled several times a year: cruises to Alaska and the Caribbean, driving trips to New Orleans and the desert, and Christmas trips to New York City and Williamsburg, Virginia.

What would he do now at Christmastime? What would Thanksgiving and Christmas be without Mary Margaret? There were no relatives he was very close to, either on his side of the family or hers. He had little interest now in playing golf, gourmet dinners or bridge. He launched a reading campaign, attacking many of the classics he had neglected in college and had little time for in his working life.

George tired of reading. He could not concentrate on the pages in front of him. He needed to make some changes in things and now was a good time. He sat at his desk and leafed through page after page of the document before him. The text was in his computer software and could be edited and revised with little effort. So that is exactly what he did.

He changed several paragraphs in the document and printed out two new copies. He took them to his bank and had his signature notarized. He placed one signed, dated and notarized copy in a flat envelope, addressed to William W. Crawford, attorney at law.

George did not arrive at the Plantation Club dining room at the appointed time. LaKisha stayed near the door watching for him. Finally, she took the bourbon Manhattan back to the bar and attended to the needs of other customers. George did not eat dinner at the Plantation Club every weekday night, and it was not unusual for him to miss two or three evenings in a row when going off island for dinner with friends. LaKisha assumed he was on a short trip. Still, her evening shift didn't seem quite the same without George at the window table. She missed their evening chats.

He was absent all week and LaKisha began to worry. When the third week went by without a sign of her friend she looked in The Landings telephone directory for a number. Uncertain as to whether it was appropriate for her to call a club member, she dialed the number anyway. The phone had been disconnected.

Toward the end of a third month of his absence the Plantation Club manager summoned LaKisha to her office.

"There's a telephone call for you," she said. "If it's personal business don't be long, we are expecting a big crowd tonight."

LaKisha took the phone and waited for the manager to leave. "Hello."

"Is this LaKisha Marie Barber?" It was a man's voice, deep and authoritative.

"Yes, it is."

"My name is William Crawford, and I am an attorney with the firm Wilson, Randolph and Crawford. I understand you are acquainted with a Mr. George R. Wardlaw, a resident at The Landings on Skidaway Island?"

"Well, yes, I know him," she answered. "He was a regular here at the restaurant where I'm a waitress. But I haven't seen him for over three months now."

"I am sorry to have to report this," he said, "Mr. Wardlaw died of a heart attack and my firm is handling the disposition of his estate."

LaKisha took a deep breath, trying to compose herself. She wanted to cry but couldn't. George was one of the reasons she found it easy to come to a second job after being on her feet for hours at a Kroger's cash register. She did not have the benefit of a father's love and guidance. The older men in their neighborhood were of no assistance, and she had only had one or two male teachers in high school. In those brief evening conversations, George Wardlaw had offered something she had not experienced from a man: an understanding acceptance of her as a person, a genuine interest that was not possessive and which required nothing in return accept kindness. Now this very nice man, a gentleman who had been so thoughtful, was no more. How many more things could go wrong in her life?

"Would it be possible for you to come to my office on Barnard Street next Friday afternoon at 2:00 P.M.?"

"What for?" she asked, uncertain as to his motive and her involvement in anything having to do with an attorney or Mr. Wardlaw's death.

"It would be very important for you to do so," he added. "And please bring with you a birth certificate, if you have it, your Social Security number and a current driver's license with photo ID."

"Why would I need all that?" she asked.

"Just trust me, young lady, it will be very important for you to be there with the proper identification."

He gave LaKisha the address of his law firm and she wrote it on a pad by the telephone. Then she sat down next to the desk and held her head in her hands, giving way to huge sobs. George was dead. This was the first person to die that she had known so closely, talked with almost every day. She felt slightly sick to her stomach and didn't know how long she had been sitting there before the manager called her back to the dining room. It would be a long and difficult evening. There were so few people in her life to offer hope and encouragement, and now a special one of them was gone. *Life is not fair,* she thought. *What good does it do to believe in angels?*

LaKisha managed to take time away from the Kroger job and arrived at the Barnard street address on schedule She found the law firm name and floor number. A secretary greeted her and ushered her into a conference room with several people she did not recognize, none of whom bothered to acknowledge her presence.

After a series of preliminary announcements, Mr. Crawford began reading aloud the Last Will and Testament of George R. Wardlaw. Toward the end the will included a gift to LaKisha M. Barber in the amount of $75,000, for the purpose of supporting expenses during college attendance. In addition, a full scholarship, including tuition and books had been established at Armstrong Atlantic University in the name of LaKisha Marie Barber for studies toward a degree in nursing.

LaKisha was stunned. She could not speak. She had trouble breathing. For a long moment she sat in a daze as the people in the room watched for a reaction. Big tears rolled down her cheeks. "There truly are angels," she said out loud. "I do believe in angels."

A Better Looking Corpse

Fowler Corners, Mississippi
Population: 4,842

He looked around his apartment, thinking he needed to pick up the clothes scattered in the spare bedroom and make certain there were no dirty dishes in the sink. On second thought, what did it matter? People could just think whatever they wanted when they found him missing.

He walked south from his apartment building, heading to the railroad track crossing six blocks away. Once on the track he walked along at a slow, deliberate pace, carefully stepping from one crosstie to the next. He was on his way to a trestle over Fowler Creek about a half mile down the track. Hands deep in his pockets, collar up against the cold morning air, Joe Edward Crawford's mind was elsewhere. He was struggling with a series of issues. The decision to take this final step came sometime after midnight, during another sleepless night, his fifth in a row. He was fed up with his life, confused about his former girlfriend's departure, disappointed in his brother, exhausted from thinking about it, and resolved that the whole of it was not worth the pain and agony. Tired of feeling like a loser, he was certain the railroad track and the trestle would be high enough to accomplish his objective.

The several months leading to this day were filled with the most intense soul searching of his forty-two years of life. What can you do when the woman you lived with for several years just leaves without so much as a good-bye, not even a note? She just packed her things while he was at work and disappeared. Then, too, he felt a strong sense of betrayal by his own brother, someone he had always looked up to and trusted. The more he thought about it, the whole of his life and his future simply added up to a big, fat zero.

Joe Ed, as he was known in Fowler Corners, had always been referred to as Troy Crawford's younger brother. Troy was the family's fair-haired boy, the high school quarterback, president of his senior class, and the scholar who was chosen by classmates as Most Likely To Succeed. He was the one to go on to college at Mississippi State and earn a degree in business administration. He joined one of Mississippi's largest real estate firms, headquartered in the nearby Capital City of Jackson. Troy was well-known at the time as a state football hero and could attract business on his name alone. He was the carefree bachelor, entertaining the ladies, living the good life.

Joe Ed graduated from Fowler Corners High School in 1946, two years behind his brother. He was tired of school and the books, never even considered college. After his obligatory two years in the U.S. Army, he went to work for the Fowler Corners Post Office. That was nineteen years ago.

His brother Troy had attended Mississippi State on a full athletic scholarship, earning the starting quarterback position in his junior year. The local weekly newspaper, the *Fowler Weekly Report*, did a glowing feature on Troy, predicting extraordinary things in the classroom and on the football field. The morning daily in Jackson, the *Clarion-Ledger*, published a full-page sports feature about his exploits on the gridiron. These all helped in the early success of his real estate sales business. Over time, however, people did not remember his name as a sports star and he had to compete on a level playing field with other agents in the business.

Joe Ed looked down at the water in Fowler Creek, 150 to 200 feet below the train trestle. He had finally come to grips with the truth: There was really nothing more to interest him. Here he was single, now over forty, still a rural mail carrier in a nowhere small town. The decision to end it all had seemed easier back in his apartment. Here on the railroad bridge he needed to think on it awhile. He needed to make certain this was the right thing. He was sitting on the side of the trestle, having no clue as to how long he had been there when a figure appeared at the far turn of the track. He could make out the form of a man walking toward him and carrying a duffle bag.

Joe Ed glanced over his shoulder, taking an occasional peek as the stranger grew closer and closer. The man wore ankle-high boots, ragged blue jeans and a dirty brown jacket. His slouch hat was tilted to the right and he carried the bag over his shoulder. Joe Ed had seen bums near the railroad track before. This one was a genuine bum if ever he had seen one.

The stranger spoke as he approached. "Good morning!"

"Morning."

"How you doing?" he asked.

"Okay," replied Joe Ed.

The disheveled stranger stopped beside him and dropped his bag to the ground.

"Mind if I sit a spell?"

"It's a free country. Sit if you want."

That's how it began. That's how the distraught Joe Ed Crawford met the down-and-out hobo William Randolph Simpson. Neither man spoke for a time. They both looked over the edge of the railroad bridge, watching the water flow below them.

"It's a bit chilly," observed the bum, "but otherwise a very nice day, don't you think?"

"Not really," said Joe Ed.

"Are you having a bad day, my friend? " asked the stranger.

"I'm not your friend, and what kind of day I'm having is my own business."

"Well, excuse me for living! Just trying to be friendly and thought you might could use some help."

The silence lasted longer this time, then Joe Ed looked over at him. "I really don't need help from a bum."

"Wait a minute, I am not a bum. I'm a hobo!" The stranger was offended. "There's a difference you know."

Joe Ed was grinning now, finding this reaction somewhat amusing. Somehow it struck him as humorous: a hobo not a bum. He was suddenly curious about the stranger, forgetting his own problems for the moment.

"Okay, what's the difference?" he asked.

"A bum is on the road, begging for pocket change or food, with no skills and no prospects. He is out there because he has to be, not by choice. A hobo is riding the rails because he wants to, doing research, discovering the country, exploring the scenery, making the decision to live the life of a nomad."

"So, how is it you're a hobo and not a bum?"

"A hobo has talent, education, skills and is of a much higher class. Believe it or not, I actually have a Ph.D. in English from the University of Missouri, and taught American and English literature at the University of Arkansas.

"So, should I be calling you professor?"

"Ask me any question you want about James Joyce, Thomas Wolf, Jane Austen, Thomas Hardy, Thoreau, Melville or . . ."

"Okay, okay, whiz kid. If you're so skilled and educated, why are you bumming, or hoboing around like this?"

"It's usually one of two reasons," he explained. "It's almost always woman troubles or booze, sometimes both. In my case it was the booze."

"How so?"

"I took a liking to good Kentucky bourbon. At first I drank to be social at faculty dinners and get-togethers. Then I drank to relax and feel better. Finally, I drank just to get drunk. Over time that caused me to lose my job and my career. In the college ranks, that kind of reputation rattles behind you like a tin can tied to your tail."

"Sorry to hear that."

"What about you? A woman or booze?"

"Neither." He threw a pebble over the side and listened for the splash below. "I'm just a loser with nowhere to go from here. I'm just fed up with being an average person."

"There's no such thing as an average person, each human is a unique individual."

"I'm a pathetically average human."

"Couldn't be . . .," added the professor. "A truly average human would have just one tit and one testicle."

Joe Ed's grin turned into genuine laughter. The absurdity of the imagery presented by his uninvited guest was too much.

"Were you thinking about taking a head-first dive off this bridge?" asked the professor.

"How did you know?"

"I've been riding the rails and sleeping in hobo camps for ten months. I've seen lots of people who felt down and out. It's something you sense more than see."

"Well, Professor, you sensed this one right."

For some reason, Joe Ed felt at ease talking with the professor, telling him things even his fellow post office workers didn't know. What did it matter, he was planning to end it all that afternoon anyway.

"Tell you what," offered the professor, "when you get ready to jump, just let me know and I'll jump with you."

"Why would you do that?"

"I'm about at the end of my rope too, getting tired of this life, no real plan for a future. Might as well get it over with."

There followed another long period of silence, broken finally by a train whistle in the distance. After a minute or two, the second blast told them the train was approaching from the north.

"When was the last time you had anything to eat?" asked Joe Ed.

"I guess from about this time yesterday, or maybe the day before over in Louisiana."

"Are you hungry?"

"Sure, just about all the time."

"How 'bout some bacon and eggs."

"Sounds good to me, but weren't we about ready to jump off this bridge?"

"We can come back and do that this afternoon. I have some stuff in the refrigerator that I would hate to waste."

The unlikely duo scrambled to their feet and proceeded back down the track toward Fowler Corners. Joe Ed walked again on the cross ties, carefully stepping from one to another. William, the professor, shuffled along beside the track with his bag slung over his shoulder. Joe Ed's apartment building was four blocks from the intersection and his unit was on the ground floor.

William took off his muddy boots at the door. Joe Ed invited him into the kitchenette and put on a pot of coffee. It was a small two-bedroom place, modestly furnished. A small sitting room also had a dinette and kitchen at one end. William looked around and noticed that there were no family photos anywhere. He started to ask why, then thought better of it.

"How do you like your eggs?" Joe Ed asked.

"Scrambled. Actually, any way will be fine. They say beggars can't be choosers."

"What abut hobos?" Joe Ed said with a chuckle, impressed by his choice of words.

"Neither can hobos."

Joe Ed rummaged around in his refrigerator, looking for an open container of mayhaw jelly. He wanted the jelly with wheat toast, important items for his last meal on earth. He found it and soon had placed plates of bacon, toast and eggs on the table. Next he poured two cups of steaming hot coffee.

"Thank you very much," said William. "This is the best-looking food I have seen in a long time. Around the rail yards and hobo camps we usually end up with cans of potted meat, Vienna sausage or Spam. Hot coffee is a special treat."

The two ate and talked, and talked and talked. They lost track of time. Joe Ed explained that he had lived with a girlfriend for three years, a nurse at Fowler General. A month ago she simply announced she had taken a job in New Orleans and left. She didn't leave a forwarding address, not even a telephone number. He had seen or heard nothing from her since. That had been a severe bruise to his ego.

Joe Ed's parents were dead. His mother died six years earlier and his father eight months ago. His father was a hard, no-nonsense type guy, very domineering. Even his brother Troy, the star of the family, did not cross his father. Thirty years before, Mr. Crawford began buying small tracts of bottomland near Fowler Creek. Any extra funds the family had went into land, dictated by the father's wishes. His favorite saying was: "It's the one thang they ain't making no more of!" Over time he had accumulated just over 2,000 acres. After his wife's death, he sold a large tract of the land to the Tupelo Power & Light Company, making a handsome profit and making way for the building of a large hydroelectric plant near the river.

Troy, the successful real estate agent, was named executor of his father's estate, now amounting to several million dollars. Joe Ed expected the holdings to be divided evenly between the sons. He was counting on that to be able to retire in style and fulfill a lifelong dream. Trouble was, shortly after the father's death, Troy sold his condo in the State Capital, moved out and disappeared. Joe Ed had tried everything he knew to find him. Phone disconnected, no forwarding address, nothing! He had no idea where Troy went, what happened to the estate, or what to do about it. He told the professor all about this as they sat at the dining table drinking coffee.

"You need to hire a lawyer and go after him," suggested the professor.

"I would need a private detective just to find him, then a lawyer to follow up with some kind of action. I know this kind of thing can drag on for years. I don't want to sue Troy! I don't have the stomach for it, even if I could afford it, which I can't. It's just so hard to think your own brother would run out on you like that!"

"What would you do with such an inheritance?"

Joe Ed told of his hobby of reading travel catalogues, dreaming of seeing exotic places when he retired. He wanted to spend time in England, France and Austria. He had read all about the many things to see and do there. His half of the land money would allow him to travel extensively throughout Europe and more. Now, that didn't seem possible.

"I have a closet full of clothes I won't be needing anymore, and we both are about the same size. Why don't you go in there and pick out some slacks and a shirt, take a hot bath and shave."

"Why would I need to do that if we're going back to jump off that bridge?"

"'Cause," he grinned, "it would make you a better looking corpse."

"Well, I guess you do have a point there."

"You may be a hobo but you look and smell like a bum!"

The professor laughed out loud as he disappeared into the bathroom and soon Joe Ed could hear water running. He went to his closet and took out several pairs of pants, shirts and shoes. He was beginning to enjoy the professor's company, losing the tension he had felt for months in his neck and shoulders. He picked out a nice outfit and placed the clothes across his bed.

The professor emerged from the bathroom, powdered, clean-shaven and sporting a towel around his waist. He discarded the ragged clothes, and then changed into clean khaki pants and a bright red polo shirt. He still needed a haircut, but the shave and bath, combined with clean clothing, made him appear ready to return to the classroom, poised to lecture about Herman Melville or John Steinbeck.

"Go look in the mirror," said Joe Ed. "Tell me what you think."

The professor returned from the bathroom mirror with a huge grin on his face.

"I don't know how to thank you," he said. "I haven't felt this good in months."

"Neither have I," said Joe Ed. "Why don't we celebrate. Do you like barbeque?"

"Sure I do, but didn't we plan to go jump off that bridge this evening?"

"We can do that in the morning. But tonight let's go out to River Rats, the best barbeque place this side of the Mississippi."

Joe Ed and the professor got in Joe Ed's vintage Ford Mustang convertible and drove to the restaurant. It was especially busy on a Friday night. They ordered full rib dinners with all the works. Joe Ed ordered a beer, but the professor stuck with sweet tea. He had been away from bourbon for months, but still battled the desire. For some reason he didn't quite understand, it was much easier to resist the booze while enjoying a great meal and conversation with Joe Ed. With extra orders of bread and coleslaw, and with sticky fingers, they talked and talked and talked, finding it comfortable sharing stories about their past.

The professor told of his upbringing in St. Louis, the son of a successful father and talented mother. His father was general counsel for a large insurance company and his mom played violin with the St. Louis Symphony. As an only child, he was denied nothing material, but his parents were not very affectionate, pushing him hard with high expectations of academic excellence. So, he did excel at his studies. He didn't have any close friends and did not participate in any sports or extracurricular activities. He had his pick of top universities and earned both his undergraduate and master's degrees at Washington University in St. Louis. The Ph.D. in English came easy at the University of Missouri, where he specialized in the classics. He had a number of choice opportunities to teach in top colleges and universities. He was a popular professor at the University of Arkansas, but cultural and educational stimuli outside the university were limited in Fayetteville. He soon found himself in the narrow, limiting and somewhat monotonous role of a single, dedicated professor. He prepared lesson plans, lectured, graded papers, wrote articles for literary magazines and read. He read almost every book listed as a best seller in the *New York Times*. In spite of that he found himself extremely bored. Then came the booze problem. Within a year he was out of a job and his academic reputation had suffered a fatal blow.

They got back to Joe Ed's apartment around midnight; both stuffed with barbeque and tired. He ushered the professor into the spare bedroom and enlisted his help in clearing books, cloths and folders off the bed. Still, it was a special treat to sleep in a real bed after many nights in hobo camps along the railroad or in shelters in towns along the Missouri River. He said good night and climbed under the covers, sound asleep before Joe Ed left the room.

Joe Ed couldn't sleep. He replayed over and over the strange events of the day. Dozens of questions floated in and out of his head. Had he really wanted to jump off that bridge? Why had he remained so long on the railroad trestle, waiting and thinking? Was it normal to be so unsure about dying? He was uncertain about his feelings for the departed lady roommate. Did she really mean that much to him? Was his half of the family money all that important? Did some higher power bring the hobo to sit beside him and offer to jump with him? Why did he feel such an instant connection with the professor? Why had he told him so much: thoughts about his life, his fears, dreams and aspirations? Just being able to talk with the professor about so many things made him consider that somewhere deep inside he didn't really want to end his life. Maybe death was not what he was looking for. Maybe he just needed some larger resources for dealing with his pain and disappointment. Finally, sleep came, a deep, much-needed, and satisfying sleep.

Joe Ed slept late into Saturday morning, waking finally to the smell of coffee brewing. The events of the previous day came rushing at him as he sat up on the side of the bed and tried to rub the cobwebs from his eyes. Had all that really happened, or had he dreamed it. The coffee smell brought him back to reality and the fact that the professor actually existed and was preparing breakfast in his own kitchen.

Clean-shaven and neatly dressed, William Simpson brought a fresh cup of coffee into Joe Ed.

"Good morning, sunshine," he said. "Hope you slept as well as I did."

"It took me awhile, but I finally did get to sleep."

"I made breakfast. Hope that was all right with you?"

"Sure."

"I'm a grateful guest in your home, and I don't think it appropriate for me to overstay my welcome. It was very kind and thoughtful of you to take me in and provide clean clothes, a bath and more good food than I have had in months. That's also the best night's sleep I have had in a very long time. I should be moving on and getting our of your way."

"No, no!" said Joe Ed. "I'm not ready for you to go. I was able to talk with you in a way I haven't with anybody in a long time. You are a good listener and I'm sorry I burdened you with all my troubles."

"It wasn't a burden to me."

"Well, I know you didn't really mean it when you said you would jump with me off the bridge, but that caused me to think through the whole idea of ending my own life. I believe you had a hidden motive in saying that, and I want to know what it was."

"I actually meant it," said the professor. "I was ready to jump. In fact, I'm still ready to jump!"

"We need to think that through some more."

"Why don't we try some breakfast first before these pancakes get cold? The coffee is on so let's take a break from the philosophical musings this morning."

They sat down at the table, dug into the breakfast as though they hadn't stuffed themselves on barbecue the night before. They applied generous portions of butter and maple syrup on the pancakes and large slices of ham disappeared quickly. William offered to clean the dishes but Joe Ed would not hear of it. They busied themselves around the apartment, Joe Ed with the dishes and William picking up clothes and taking out the trash. It was as if neither one wanted to open the discussion about the events of the previous day or what their next move would be.

They both jumped when the doorbell rang. Joe Ed went to the door, expecting nobody on a Saturday morning. Standing before him in a green and blue cap was a Federal Express deliveryman.

"I'm looking for a Mr. Joe Edward Crawford. Is this the right address?"

"That would be me."

"I have a package for you and it's registered. I need your signature.

Please sign on the line where the X is."

Joe Ed signed the form, took the package and thanked him. It was a large FedEx envelope and had been sent from a Memphis, Tennessee, address. The professor watched as Joe Ed opened the package and took out a multi-page document.

"I don't believe this," said Joe Ed. "It's from my brother."

He read aloud.

Dear Joe Ed:

I apologize for not contacting you since Dad's death. As executor of the estate, I have been in a three-month struggle with lawyers, investment bankers and accountants who all seemed intent on giving me a hard time. All of them had other ideas about what we should do with these assets. I quit my job, sold my condo in Jackson and escaped to Memphis to try and sort this all out. It has been an unbelievable nightmare. I know I should have been in contact with you, but I just screwed up in that regard. I finally won the battle with the lawyers, letting them know that I would do things precisely as our father had expected me to.

Attached is a certified accounting statement outlining exactly where every penny of the family estate went, including all fees and taxes. Your half of the settlement comes to $987,483.60. That amount has been wired to your bank account at Fowler Corners Federal. Dad left your account number and one of your canceled checks in with his instructions. You can now retire, as I know you had been planning to do. I suggest you hire a fee-based investment specialist to help you, because you will have lots of people volunteering opinions as to what you should do with the money. Don't get involved with commissioned insurance salesmen or investment reps or brokers. They will all have "just the right" financial products for you to buy. Believe me, I have learned that lesson the hard way.

As for now, I am exhausted. Handling this distribution

has just about done me in.

So, when you read this I will already be in Singapore with my new lady friend, Myra Hampton. I have finally found the right girl. She is terrific. We are making marriage plans, but first we are leaving to sail the South China Sea for several months. Afterwards, we'll return to Memphis where I have arranged to set up my own real estate sales business. Hope you can come visit us in Memphis when we get back. I would like to introduce Myra to you in person.

Again, I am deeply sorry I did not let you know where I was and what I was doing. Hope you aren't too upset with me.

All good wishes, your exhausted brother,

Troy

Joe Ed went to the couch and sat down, holding the documents in his lap. He appeared unable to move. The blood had drained from his cheeks.

"Are you all right?" asked the professor.

"Yep. I just felt a little faint. I was thinking how close I came yesterday to missing out on all this."

"You're going to be fine now," said the professor. "I'm going to gather up my stuff and head back to the rails. I want to thank you for everything. I have really enjoyed being with you these last two days."

Joe Ed left the couch and poured himself another cup of coffee.

"Professor," he said in a loud new voice, "will you please sit back down."

The professor sat.

"Have you ever been to London?"

"I have, but that was more than a decade ago."

"Have you ever been to France or Austria?"

"No."

"Well, we're going! You are going to be my tour guide with all your education and superior book learning. I want you to handle all the travel arrangements and I want you to teach me all about the most famous English and American authors. You are going to educate me.

We are going to tour Europe for as long as we want to, and we are going to take in all the sights."

"Are you serious?"

"I am indeed. For starters we're fixin' to climb the Eiffel Tower, we're fixin' to see the Arc de Triomphe and the Louvre, and we might even stroll up and down the Champs-Elysees."

"I thought we were going back to the railroad trestle today and jump."

"Nope, not today. . . . We can do that when we get back."

A Merciful Heart

Calico Springs, Arkansas
Population: 5,887

Jake sat on the top step of the porch, staring out across the cornfield and listening to the tinkling cowbells. The sound was distinctive and soothing in the summer air. The last rays of the sun faded slowly behind a stand of large Chinaberry bushes in back of his grandfather's barn. Elbows on his knees, Jake cradled his chin in his hands and was lost for a time in deep thought, trying to imagine what the rest of his life would be like. He could not think of a single person he knew who had experienced his bad luck, certainly not anyone his age.

Jake Ryder was twelve years old. His real name was Wallace Jacob Ryder, but everyone in Calico Springs called him Jake. As the only child of Fayrene and Marvin Ryder, life had been just about ideal. His father had been the fire chief of Calico Springs, the county seat of Winston County, and young Jake had the run of the place.

He rode his bike with friends in town, went fishing at the town branch, played baseball in the vacant lot next to the fire station, spending as much time as he could out on his grandpa Ryder's farm. His grandfather, seventy-two-year-old Jay Randolph Ryder, lived alone on family acreage just beyond the city limits. Winston County, a farming region in the southeastern part of Arkansas, is nestled on the edge of the Mississippi Delta.

Jake's world changed on an April evening eighteen months ago. His parents died in a head-on collision with a large log truck. They were on the way home from a church potluck luncheon. He had gone to live with his grandpa until things could be worked out.

Grandpa Ryder had been collecting cowbells for decades, tying them to the branches of a large sweet gum tree at the corner of his yard. Friends and neighbors knew of his interest and presented him with additional cowbells found at yard sales and auctions, or those discovered in old barns. The bells were of different sizes and shapes. When evening breezes crossed the fields and into the trees, a cacophony of unusual harmonies filled the air. With the wind from the southeast, the sounds of ringing cowbells traveled across several acres toward a few neighboring houses. Some folks complained about Jay Randolph Ryder's makeshift wind chimes, declaring the sound annoying. Others thought it charming. For Jake, it was a special kind of peaceful music that helped him relax and think.

When his parents died Jake felt lost and confused, and for a time he could think of no good reason to keep on living. He only felt safe after moving to the farm with his grandfather. There are times when a twelve-year-old boy needs someone special to talk with. His grandfather had always understood him, had been more patient in explaining things, and was a much better listener than his own parents.

After the funeral and all the kind words of friends and neighbors, people went on about their lives. Distant cousins and others tried to get old Mr. Ryder to move in from the farm and live in the former fire chief's house. Grandpa Ryder and Jake talked it over, and Jake had a full grown-up person's say in the matter. They both agreed that the farm was where they needed to be. The town home held too many memories and would make the transition far too difficult.

"Why does God let good people die like that?" Jake asked.

Grandpa Ryder was quiet for a time. Then he spoke softly, almost as if talking to the wall in front of him. "I gave up trying to second guess God a long time ago," he said. "Your father was a terrific person. He was a good boy and an even better man. When he married your mother I was very proud. Your mother was a smart and beautiful lady. And when they announced that you were soon to arrive in this world, I was a very happy person."

"Everybody else I know at school still has parents," said Jake with a familiar lump forming in his throat, "except Johnny Fuller and his daddy just left one morning and never came back."

"I'm not going to blame God," said his grandfather, "but I am going to thank Him for all the many good years we had with your mom and dad. Maybe someday we can sort out the rest of it."

Jake had very little association with his maternal grandparents. They were much older and lived in an assisted living community near Savannah. His parents had met while his father was stationed at Hunter Army Air Field on the Georgia Coast. He had seen the other grandparents only once or twice. They were not able to travel and his parents had only taken a motor trip to the East Coast twice in his decade of life. He was too young to remember the first trip and could barely remember the second. The other grandmother died before he was born. Grandpa Ryder lived alone at the farm, and Jake spent as much time there as in Calico Springs.

Summer arrived just in time. Jake was a good student and enjoyed school, but the summertime and activities with Grandpa Ryder were even more important at this stage of life, and time alone on the front porch seemed ideal when he needed to think.

He looked up from his thoughts at the familiar sound of an auto approaching. Grandpa Ryder turned in off the highway and drove his Ford pickup all the way into the garage at the back of the house. Jake thought that odd since he usually left the truck parked outside under a large oak tree. He left the porch and started around the house to investigate.

Grandpa Ryder was walking back from the garage with a small dog in his arms and a huge grin on his face. "Thought we might could use a new friend," he said, holding the puppy up for Jake to see.

Jake ran to his grandfather and took the small dog in his arms. It was a collie puppy, easily mistaken for an offspring of Lassie. It looked up at Jake, licked his cheek and they became instant buddies.

"It was one of a litter of three from the collie that Wilson Doggett had at the old Radford place out near the sawmill," said his grandfather. "Mr. Doggett was giving them away to anyone who promised a good home."

"I'll make sure he has a good home," said Jake. "Thank you, Grandpa, for the puppy. Ain't he just beautiful?"

"Well," offered Grandpa Ryder, "you better learn how to tell the difference, since he is actually a she."

"Really?" Jake put the puppy on the ground and watched it with new interest. "I guess I better come up with a girl's name instead of what I was thinking."

Over the days that followed Jake and the puppy were inseparable. They ran in the fields and played hide-and-seek in the barn. He named her Daisy. Where that name came from he hadn't a clue, she just seemed like a "Daisy" to him. There was, however, one major problem. The young Daisy howled at night, a long, low, mournful howl. Jake went out to comfort her, taking extra food, and tried everything he could think of to keep the pup quiet. Nothing worked. She howled at different, unexpected times during the night, waking Grandpa Ryder and Jake alike.

Two neighbors spoke to Grandpa Ryder about it. Rufus Burk, the resident curmudgeon who lived in the nearest farmhouse to the east, approached him at the feed store and told him his wife Norma Louise could not sleep with that dog howling every night. He had a few pointed remarks to offer, suggesting strongly something be done about it, and soon.

"If you can't take care of the problem, Jay, I can!"

Rufus Burk's admonitions and the indirect threat had a nasty tone to them, and did not sit well with Grandpa Ryder.

Mrs. Darlene Rayford from the house across the road talked to him in the produce section of Wilson's Supermarket, asking if the dog was sick or in pain. She allowed as how the constant howling was getting on her nerves and causing her mother a considerable amount of tension. Could he please see to it that the dog was quiet at night?

Jake asked his grandfather if he could keep Daisy inside the house to help muffle the sound. Grandpa Ryder did not like that idea, explaining with emphasis the problems associated with a house pet. He did not want to set a precedent, since in his mind animals were to be kept outside or in the barn.

"Animals belong outdoors," he told Jake. "They need space and freedom and the farm is a perfect place for her to run and play and grow. Dogs that are kept indoors become very different and dependent, and I don't think that's what you want for Daisy."

The following evening Jake took Daisy to the barn. He carried along a pillow and blanket, intending to spend the night with his dog, hoping to keep her quiet and out of trouble with the neighbors. Daisy enjoyed the company and played with Jake until they both fell asleep. Sometime after midnight Daisy began howling, startling Jake and no doubt some of the neighbors. Jake tried to comfort the puppy and keep her quiet, realizing that he could not make this a new all-night chore. The puppy continued to howl.

Jake took the dog out and let him walk and play in the moonlight. Daisy was happy and content as long as Jake played with her. Jake couldn't think of a single thing more he could do.

Toward the end of the following week Grandpa Ryder noticed the puppy acting strangely, walking with its head down and coughing in an unusual way. He picked Daisy up and tried to look down her throat. Daisy didn't resist and went limp. Grandpa Ryder placed the dog on the ground and went to get some water. Daisy lay on her side and would not drink the water. Her breathing was labored and, at times, gasping. Then he saw a trickle of blood from the dog's mouth.

Grandpa Ryder called Jake and told him to bring a cardboard box to put the dog in.

"We need to take Daisy out to see Doc Ferrell right away," he shouted to Jake. "Get a move on, we need to hurry!"

As they pulled out of the drive Jake had all kinds of questions. "What's wrong? What's the matter with Daisy? Why do we need to go to the vet?"

Grandpa Ryder recounted his experience with the puppy and explained that he thought she was very sick. He had no idea what might have caused this. They were feeding her regular puppy chow, and she had a hardy appetite before. This morning, for some strange reason, Daisy had no energy, would not eat, had trouble breathing and appeared very ill.

Doc Ferrell was the only veterinarian in Winston County. The town folk and farmers kept him steady busy. He had a makeshift clinic in a converted barn behind his house on the west side of Calico Springs. Most of his work was with large farm animals, but a small girl with a sick kitten or a little boy with a pet rabbit got special attention.

Grandpa Ryder drove the pickup around the house and right up to the vet's clinic. He jumped out and carried the box with Daisy into the office area. Jake closed the truck doors and hurried to catch up. He was quiet. He was also scared.

Doc Ferrell stopped what he was doing and heard the plea from Grandpa and Jake. He took the dog back into another room and asked them to wait in the office.

"What could it be?" Jake asked.

"I just don't know," said Grandpa Ryder, "but it don't look good."

"Why not?"

"Daisy wasn't moving and there was some blood coming from her mouth."

Jake had a pained look on his face, trying desperately not to cry. Why do bad things always have to happen he thought? Maybe he was just jinxed. Daisy just had to get well, he had great plans for them for the remainder of the summer.

Doc Ferrell finally returned to the waiting room without Daisy. "Wallace, can I talk with you in private for a minute?"

"That's the boy's dog, Doc, I don't plan to leave him out of the news, good or bad."

"Okay then, I'm sorry to have to tell you this. I found some unusual hamburger meat in the puppy's esophagus, and I believe somebody has fed her ground glass."

Grandpa Ryder quickly put his arm around Jake's shoulders and they both choked back the urge to scream.

"Nobody would do that to a dog," exclaimed Grandpa Ryder. "I've been around a long time and I never heard of such a thing!"

Jake could hold back his feelings no longer. He ran out of the office and back to the truck, large tears streaming down his cheeks.

"The puppy is suffering something fierce," said the Doc. "I think we need to put her to down and out of her misery."

Grandpa Ryder nodded. "Thanks for your help, Doc. Just send me the bill."

"Nope, there won't be any charge. I've been treatin' animals for a long time and this is a first!"

Back home Jake went to his room and fell across his bed. He sobbed his heart out for what seemed a very long time. Why would anyone do that to an innocent little dog? Jake couldn't imagine anything worse. Grandpa Ryder left him alone, understanding too well that there are some pains that have to work themselves out. He knew that mere words would not help.

The next day Jake went to the barn and began looking for anything that might suggest how and why Daisy was given meat with broken glass in it. He thought maybe the puppy had gotten into house garbage, but he and Grandpa Ryder had not cooked any hamburger meat for weeks, and there was no broken glass anywhere near the trash barrel outside.

There were trails leading from behind the barn to the Burk house across the way, and a second trail around the barn, used by farmhands who came to work for his grandfather on a piecemeal basis. Perhaps one of the workers gave Daisy some bad meat, or could it be Rufus Burk who had made both a fuss and a threat about the howling at night.

Jake followed the trail to the Burk place, inspecting both sides of the path in search of any evidence of such a misdeed. The Burk house was set back from the road, with a pair of large magnolia trees in the front yard. The garage was detached and located west of the house. Mr. Burk used the garage for farm equipment, primarily a small tractor used for work in his garden. He parked his black Chevy pickup truck between the garage and the house, a fact that annoyed Norma Louise no end. The back yard had a water faucet sticking out of the ground some distance from the house and a birdbath on the ground under the faucet. At the back of the yard was a wire fence surrounding Mr. Burk's garden.

As Jake approach he could see Mr. Burk gathering sticks from his yard and placing them in a pile at the back of his garden. He was obviously planning another bonfire, something he did frequently to the dismay of the Calico Springs Fire Department. He was supposed to notify them before any burning of trash or leaves, but he was negligent in doing so.

Jake watched the process from a crouched position halfway down the path. Soon Mr. Burk left the yard and entered the screen porch at the back of his house. Jake moved in closer and waited until he heard and saw no movement. He ran to the edge of the garden and found what he was looking for at the bottom of the steps leading to the Burk back porch.

Jake moved around to the trash container and opened the lid. He began moving things around inside until he found the plastic wrapper for ground beef, packaged by Quality Meats, Inc. of Little Rock, Arkansas. There was no way to match the package with the hamburger given to Daisy, but he took the package anyway and stuffed it in his pocket.

On the way back to the trail he spied a broken windshield from an old farm tractor. Someone had stomped the safety glass and smashed it into several small pieces at one end. There might be a way to match the glass with that given to Daisy, so he put some in his pocket and ran back down the trail toward home.

He knew Grandpa Ryder would not like him snooping around the Burk place, so he kept quiet about what he had found. More than ever, he was convinced that old Mister Burk had put ground glass in hamburger meat and fed it to his puppy.

The following evening, Jake stayed awake until his grandfather was in bed asleep. He eased out of the back screen door and made his way to the barn. He placed six concrete blocks in a wheelbarrow, as well as a long-handle tire jack from his grandfather's garage.

The Rufus Burk place was dark, all the lights out and it appeared that Rufus and Norma Louise had gone to bed.

Jake rolled the wheelbarrow up to the back of Mr. Burk's Chevy pickup. As quiet as could be, he jacked the right rear axle up just high enough to place three of the blocks underneath. He performed the exact same task on the left wheel, leaving the truck's back tires suspended one inch above the ground.

Jake was not around to witness the events of the following morning, but Rufus Burk left home early, climbing into his pickup for a trip to town. He started the engine and eased it into gear. He pushed the gas pedal and heard the engine speed up. Strangely enough, the truck didn't move. He put the gear in reverse and again applied the gas. The engine responded but the truck did not. Mr. Burk got out and opened the hood, looking inside as if he might actually see something wrong. He walked around the vehicle and saw nothing unusual. Back in the cab he started the engine and experienced the same result. He slammed the truck door as he exited the vehicle and went inside to call Ralph Boland, the mechanic at the Calico Springs Exxon Station just off Main Street. Ralph promised to come out to look at the truck as soon as he could.

Later in the morning Ralph arrived in his service van with a new sign painted on the side: CALICO SPRINGS EXXON. He talked briefly with Mr. Burk, climbed in the cab of the Chevy and started the engine. A big grin crossed his face as he listened to the wheels spin. He stepped out of the cab and looked under the back of the truck, letting out a big belly laugh at what he saw. "You been driving on air, Rufus," he said with a guffaw. "Somebody has played a good trick on you!"

Rufus Burk didn't think it was funny one bit, vowing to get even with anyone who would play such a prank.

"I ain't charging you nothing for this call, Rufus, but don't call me again 'til you have done more investigatin' on your part. From what I hear at the station, could be some dog owners don't like you that much. If you done what the rumor says you done, wouldn't be surprised if you have more serious pranks coming on."

That remark stung Rufus. He didn't know what to say. He had heard some of the rumors going around about his involvement with the loss of Jake's dog. His conscience was now giving him serious pain. With that, Ralph headed back to the service station for an afternoon of oil and grease jobs. He had also promised Maebell Bloodworth that he would change the head gasket in her ancient Desoto.

The next morning Grandpa Ryder prepared a breakfast of scrambled eggs, ham and hot homemade biscuits, carefully avoiding any mention of Daisy and the horrible deed done to her.

Jake finally brought up the subject. "I found these a couple of days ago over at Mr. Burk's house." He held up the meat wrapper and glass pieces.

Grandpa Ryder inspected the items and took a deep breath. "It sure looks suspicious but that wouldn't be clear enough evidence for certain that Rufus Burk did it."

"But I know he did," said Jake.

"Let me have that stuff and tomorrow I'll have a long talk with Sheriff Robinson. In the meantime, don't you be going near the Rufus Burk place again, you hear?"

"Yes, sir."

That afternoon Grandpa Ryder drove into town and to the sheriff's office just off the town square. Sheriff Robinson had been in office for twelve years, a stabilizing fixture in local government. He was a very imposing figure, standing six feet four and 260 pounds. In Calico Springs he was large enough to command attention and respect. Gary Wayne Robinson was a graduate of Calico Springs High School. His parents could not afford college and saw little need for higher education anyway. So, Gary worked at a local sawmill for ten years before deciding to run for sheriff. He was elected with a comfortable margin. The voters found him a very direct person, possessing a wealth of common sense, and very little sympathy for troublemakers. Where the sheriff stood on most local issues was never a subject for lengthy debate.

The sheriff listened to Grandpa Ryder's version of the incident and studied carefully the items he brought.

"Not enough to prove that Rufus Burk killed your dog," he told Grandpa Ryder, "even though I'm pretty sure he had something to do with it. Do you have any other evidence?"

Grandpa Ryder explained that it was all they had to go on, except the veiled threat old Mister Burk had delivered before the dog died.

Somehow the rumor leaked out in Calico Springs that Rufus Burk was responsible for the death of young Jake's collie puppy.

At Parker's barbershop on Main Street, Burk was confronted by several patrons asking if he had plans for any other dogs in the county that week. He didn't know how to respond, finally just keeping his mouth shut. He couldn't bring himself to deny it.

Two women in front of the Wilson Feed & Seed, scolded him directly about harming cats and dogs, heaping such pain on innocent children.

Joe Wilson Doggett stopped Rufus Burk getting in his truck at the Save More Super Market, telling him in no uncertain terms that if he ever came near his place and his registered bird dogs, it would be the worst day of his life.

"I heard what you done to the Ryder boy's dog," he said, shaking his fist in Mr. Burk's face.

Rufus Burk had no idea how the rumor started. He realized that the information was now widespread and most of the citizens of Calico Springs had the impression he was associated with the death of Jake's puppy. His reputation was severely damaged, with neighbors now viewing him as a subhuman character, worthy of ridicule or shunning. He had enjoyed a reputation as a tough man in the county, taking no guff from anyone. That reputation was not serving him well at the moment.

Rufus felt the huge weight of this scorn by neighbors and former friends. Some women at the beauty shop had even given Norma Louise the cold shoulder. The guilt he experienced was overwhelming, so much so that he went to see Father McFarland at St. James Church, confessing his ill deed and asking forgiveness. In the process of confession the priest told him that God would surely forgive, but he needed to seek forgiveness from the community, especially that of young Jake Ryder.

Rufus Burk was in a tough spot. He didn't know how to approach Jake, or what to say. Rufus Burk had little experience asking anyone for forgiveness. He was also concerned that Jake and his grandpa might bring charges against him, or worse. Two weeks went by as he struggled with the guilt and Father McFarland's charge. Finally, he could stand it no longer. He had to do something.

Jake was again setting on the top step to the front porch, thinking to himself and listening to the cowbells chimes. Rufus Burk's pickup made the turn off the gravel road and up Grandpa Ryder's driveway. This took Jake by surprise. Why would he be coming to this house? This could be more trouble.

Jake didn't move as Mr. Burk got out of his truck and walked to the front steps. "I need to talk to you, Jake," he said. Jake nodded but didn't speak.

Mr. Burk had a worried look on his face, saying, "I have done a very bad thing."

"I know," said Jake.

"I can't explain to you just how sorry I am for what I done."

"Why did you do it?"

"I just lost my head, 'cause I ain't never ever done anything like that before. I don't know what got into me, Jake. For days now I have been disappointed in myself, then really mad at myself. That's probably the worse thing I have ever done in my life."

Jake looked at the ground and remained silent.

"I'm asking you to forgive me," he almost choked on the words. "Could you please find it in your heart to forgive me?"

After a long, thoughtful pause, Jake said, "I don't know . . . I'll have to think on it."

"Fair enough."

Mr. Burk walked back to his truck, opened the door and looked back at Jake. "I'm going to find a way to make it up to you, young feller. That's a promise. I don't know how yet, but that's a promise."

Later that evening as Grandpa Ryder and Jake sat down to a supper of potato soup and bread, Jake told him about Mr. Burk's visit and about his asking for forgiveness. Grandpa Ryder did not respond for several minutes, realizing that he needed to say the right things in this situation, expecting that young Jake would find this a valuable lesson.

"What did you tell him?"

"I said I'd need to think on it."

"Sounds to me like Mr. Burk has been having a serious battle with his conscience. What do you think?"

"I guess so," said Jake.

"I don't think Rufus Burk is an evil man, I just think he made a very bad mistake. Sounds like he is very sorry for it."

"But what do I tell him?" asked Jake.

"You have to decide that for yourself, but with his confession like that, we could call Sheriff Robinson and bring charges against him."

"What do you think would happen to him?"

"He might spend some time in jail," said Grandpa Ryder, "but it probably would mean a large fine."

"I don't think I want to bring charges," said Jake.

"Why not?"

"I'm just tired of thinking about it and tired of people talking about it. It wouldn't bring Daisy back anyway."

Grandpa Ryder took a deep breath and measured his words carefully. "All I can tell you is that being angry at someone, holding a grudge, or even trying to get even by doing something bad to that person in return is never a good idea."

"Why?"

"I just believe that if you hold on to anger, it only causes you more pain and suffering yourself. Forgiving Mr. Burk does not mean that you accept what he did as okay. Forgiveness can be a gift that you give to another person; helping you let go of feeling bad and offering peace of mind. I'm not saying all this very well, Jake, but am I making any sense?"

"Yes, Grandpa, I understand. But it still won't be easy."

"I know it won't be, but there are some things you learn by just living long enough. I'm getting to be a old man, Jake, and I have learned that anger and resentment can sometimes seem all right, even justified, so much so that you can become attached to it. Anger can change you if you hold on to it, and not for the better. Forgiveness is taking a positive action that can help you be the kind of person you want to be."

"So, what do I tell Mr. Burk?"

"You still have to make that decision for yourself."

Three days went by and Jake changed his mind several times. A few times he wanted to forgive Mr. Burk. Then there were others where he wanted to punish him and get even. Putting his back truck tires on cinder blocks was a start, but he had thought about putting sand in his gas tank. He hadn't done that because it would have done serious damage to Mr. Burk's truck, and even though he was very angry with him, he didn't really want to return that much evil. Somehow, that just didn't seem right to Jake.

On the afternoon of the third day, Jake rode his bicycle around to the Burk place. He stopped at the steps, put down his kickstand and went to the front door. Mrs. Burk came to the door before he had a chance to knock.

"Hello, Jake," she said, "is everything all right?"

"Yes, ma'am," he answered. "Can I speak to Mr. Burk?"

She nodded and called her husband. Rufus Burk put down his magazine and came to join his wife. He opened the screen door and stepped out on the porch with Jake, closing the door behind him.

"I just wanted to let you know that I have decided to forgive you," said Jake.

Rufus Burk felt a large lump form in his throat, and he was unsuccessful in holding back tears. It had been a very long time since he shed tears. He swallowed hard and it was difficult for him to speak. "Thank you, Jake," he said. "I want you to know that's really important to me, and I will keep my promise to you. You are a fine young man and you have a merciful heart."

Jake ran to his bike and peddled hard out the driveway, avoiding having to say anything more to Mr. Burk and anxious to be away from the awkward moment. He told his grandfather about his decision and about going over to see Mr. Burk.

Grandpa Ryder smiled and patted Jake on the back. "You are a very special young man," he told him. "I am very proud of you."

The summer was coming to an end. School was only days away and Jake was ready to see his classmates and get back to his studies as a member of the seventh-grade class at Calico Springs Middle School.

It was a Saturday morning and Jake had his bicycle upside down in front of the barn, oiling the wheels and the chain linkage. The county swimming pool had closed for the summer and Grandpa Ryder had talked about going to a movie that evening. That was a special outing he and his grandfather enjoyed, a big bag of buttered popcorn, Royal Crown Colas and a movie at the Calico Springs Drive-In on the Jackson highway. Grandpa Ryder had read a review of *The Yearling*, staring Gregory Peck. He was sure Jake would love this movie.

There was a steady breeze from the southeast and the cowbells created music from the front yard.

He was turning his bike back right side up when he heard a truck pull into the driveway. Mr. Burk stopped next to the house and climbed out of the cab, carefully carrying a squirming puppy in his arms.

"Here, Jake," he said grinning from ear to ear. "Thought you might like to have this little fellow as a new pet."

Jake didn't know what to say. He reached out and took the puppy in his arms.

"He ain't no collie, but he's a registered Jack Russell Terrier and comes from a good family."

The puppy was about sixteen weeks old, smaller than those bred for hunting. He had a stubby tail, set rather high, and his coat was smooth. He had a predominately white body, with and tan head and left ear. There were several black spots on his back.

He continued to squirm as Jake took him, holding him firmly as the puppy licked his face. "Thank you, Mr. Burk," was all he could think of to say.

"And Jake . . . I want you to know that I don't care one whit if the little fellow howls all night long!"

Rufus Burk seemed satisfied with himself, feeling that in some strange way he had made at least one step toward making things right. He knew that wasn't enough and he planned to find ways to do more. In the meantime, it was his best start.

Jake held the puppy high over his head, looking at his underbelly. Mr. Burk watched with curiosity and wasn't sure what the boy meant when he said, "Now I can use that boy's name I thought up before."

The Couch

Chadeau, Louisiana
Population: 12,484

Miguel Echeverria waited for his luggage at the Pan American carousel in the New Orleans International Airport. He was exhausted and impatient after traveling from Caracas with a connection in San Juan. His stay in Venezuela had been only eighteen days but the time away from his adopted home seemed longer. He hoped this was to be a last trip of this type. Within a matter of days he would be free to follow his dream.

Edie Echeverria, his father's oldest sister, an avowed old maid, gladly took Miguel in when he arrived at the New Orleans suburb two years before at age eighteen. With his parent's permission and blessing, he left Venezuela with his uncle Eduardo Esteban. Aunt Edie had agreed in advance to provide room and board in her townhouse in Chadeau, a bedroom community east of the Crescent City with an increasing Latin population. She was glad to have a young man's presence in her home, allowing her a greater connection with family, as well as an extra measure of safety and ready hands for certain chores that were now beyond her strength or reach.

"Miguel," called Edie, "could you change please the lightbulb in the kitchen ceiling?"

"Miguel," she chided, "I need you to fix the toilet seat in the bathroom downstairs."

Miguel was following a plan for an education in America, a decent job and a better life. There were few prospects for him in

Caracas, a sprawling city near the Yucatan Peninsula, teeming with a population impossible to census. The eldest son of the eight children of Isabel and Jose, Miguel had shown more ambition than his brothers and sisters. His father worked for the city government, cleaning the streets near the Zona Rosa. His mother took care of the children and earned a few pesos repairing clothes for neighbors and friends with her Singer sewing machine, the only one in their neighborhood. Miguel began in early childhood asking his parents to let him go to the United States. They were reluctant at first; eventually realizing it would mean one less mouth to feed and the possibility that Miguel could earn enough to send funds back home.

His uncle Esteban was the dandy of the family, a fancy dresser who drove new luxury cars, smoked expensive cigars and was rarely seen in the evening without the company of attractive young ladies. He was well-known as a regular at certain bars and restaurants along Bourbon and Conti streets in the French Quarter. Eduardo insisted that Miguel take a job with him until he could get on his feet in the city. With few options available, Miguel took the offer. In no time he was caught up in his uncle's business, running errands, making deliveries, and eventually taking travel assignments back and forth to Latin America. Soon Miguel was making more money than he could ever imagine growing up in the northwest barrio of Caracas. His uncle's lucrative assignments allowed him to send money home, all the while putting aside a sizable nest egg for himself.

Aunt Edie was curious about his job, asking Miguel many questions but getting only vague answers. She didn't push too far because she was impressed that he could favor her with generous gifts and treats. Miguel kept strange hours and no regular schedule. Uncle Eduardo left instructions for him on an answering machine, one he had installed and paid for. Edie listened to the messages when Miguel was away but could make no sense of them. It was as if Eduardo was speaking in code. And there were the occasional trips to San Juan and the British Virgin Islands. Miguel traveled on average about every three months, his uncle providing airline tickets and funds for limos to and from the airport.

Before leaving Caracas this last time Miguel confided to his father that he had applied for an education extension of his visa, arranging things before his current work visa ran out. He would not be back to Venezuela anytime soon and would be unable to continue frequent trips home as before. He must move on to college studies in business administration and preparation for opening his own retail store in the city. He had also begun the application process for becoming a U.S. citizen.

Although exhausted from the trip, Miguel was excited about completing this final assignment and prospects for the coming month. He knew his aunt would be disappointed in his leaving her townhouse, but she would understand his need for independence. When he returned this time, he would turn everything over to his uncle as planned. The extra bonus for this last assignment would provide enough savings for a new apartment in suburban Kenner, enrollment in night school at a nearby community college and a start for his business. Miguel had been working for months on plans for a corner market specializing in Latin American foods.

The luggage arrived. Miguel waited at curbside for the limo driver to open the trunk. He sank into the leather seat in back, smiling to himself at his good fortune. During the cab ride, Miguel almost went to sleep. When they arrived, he paid and tipped the driver and hurried up the steps. Something was different. Aunt Edie's house had a new look. There was a new coat of paint on the wood trim and the windows were clean and shining. There were new flower boxes stationed on either side of the entrance that displayed a profusion of color, accessories he had not seen before.

His aunt was waiting just inside the door. "I am so very glad you are here!" she said, greeting him with unusual enthusiasm.

"I have for you a big surprise," she gushed. "You have been so kind and helpful, I decided to surprise you with a new decoration for your room and the parlor! We have a new bed and new furniture for the whole downstairs!"

Miguel looked around the parlor and into his room, stunned by what he saw.

"Where is the sofa?" he said with a frown.

"Don't you like the new look?" said his aunt. "I had the whole downstairs painted!"

"What happened to the sofa?" he asked with a stern, deliberate tone.

"It was so old." She smiled. " I put it out with the bed frame for the trash pickup. I wanted you to have all new things."

Miguel couldn't speak. He couldn't think. He slumped down next to the stairs with his head in his hands. He could only imagine how angry his uncle would be. The big bosses would blame his uncle. They would go loco. This was going to mean unbelievable trouble.

"When did you put them out?" Miguel asked, trying hard to control his voice.

"Day before yesterday," she answered. "What's wrong, don't you like your new room?"

In an instant Miguel's plans for school, a business in America and a new life flashed and faded before his eyes. He ran into the bedroom, gathered his remaining belongings in a second suitcase, and tucked his secret money supply in his jacket, hurrying back to the parlor.

"Thank you, Aunt Edie," he said. "Thank you for everything. I'm very sorry to tell you, but I can't stay here. I have to leave right now. I'm going back to Caracas and I won't be coming back."

"What's the matter? Why are you leaving? Did I do something wrong? Tell me what's happening!"

Miguel hurried back to the street, hailed a cab, jumped in and waved good-bye to his aunt. As the cab pulled away Edie set on the stoop with big tears running down her cheeks.

Later that evening she tried to telephone Eduardo. Call after call went unanswered.

She finally left a message on his answering machine: "Eduardo, this is Edie, please call me. Something is wrong with Miguel. He's packed all his things and left. I don't know what happened. I don't know what to do. Please call me as soon as you get this message."

Edie sat on the new sofa and fought back tears. "What could be wrong with changing Miguel's room and the parlor?" she thought. "It has all new furniture for goodness sakes, much better than what I threw away!" Edie slept very little that night.

The following day, Sissy Rojas, her best friend and next-door neighbor, showed up at the usual hour to share morning coffee and conversation. Under her arm was the city section from the *Times Picayune*. A small article had caught her eye.

"Edie, Edie, my dear," she exclaimed, "I think you need to read this."

> *According to New Orleans police, sanitation workers picking up a discarded couch on East Hoover Street in the Latin Section of Chadeau yesterday, noticing a white powder coming out of it when they were compacting it in the rear of the truck. When narcotics officers were called to the scene around 1:00 p.m. they determined that the powder was cocaine, 235 pounds of it, with a street value of approximately $6 million. It is not known who put the drugs into the couch.*

Might'a Been Something I Ate

Medford, Arkansas
Population: 5,087

Doc Adams left the breakfast table, kissed his wife Marcia good-bye, closed the screen door behind him and crossed the flagstone path to the garage. All the while he fought the urge to crawl back in bed and catch up on some precious sleep. His rounds at Stafford County General had lasted two hours longer than planned the evening before. The morning schedule of appointments at the Adams Clinic would be grueling. That's what life is like when you are one of only three doctors in a county of approximately 5,000 people in Southeast Arkansas.

Winston W. Adams, M.D., was the senior of the three general practice physicians in Medford, a town straddling the two-lane strip of blacktop halfway between Jackson, Mississippi and Pine Bluff, Arkansas. He earned his medical degree in 1930 at the University of Mississippi, completed his internship at Charity Hospital in New Orleans, and returned to his hometown to fulfill a boyhood dream: establishing his own medical clinic in Safford County.

The garage held Doc Adams' only interest outside the medical practice other than the running Wednesday night poker game at the private Rooster Club. His pride and joy was a 1935 Packard convertible, two-toned cream and tan, one of the first mass-produced automobiles of the Packard Motor Company. The company made a production move in 1935 as a last-ditch effort to escape the effects of the Depression. While the Ford Motor Company was producing autos that sold for $440, Packard was known for upscale luxury cars costing more than $2,600 at the time. The Depression changed that strategy and Doc Adams purchased his convertible new for less than $1,000. It was the only one of its kind in Southeast Arkansas.

On this particular morning the worst thing happened. The classic Packard would not start. He turned the ignition switch, listening to the grinding starter. The motor did not respond. He questioned how long the battery would last.

Doc Adams stepped back out of the car, opened the hood and looked inside as if he actually could determine the problem and as if he actually knew what to do to fix it. Finally, he slammed the hood shut, kicked the tire and called his car a "miserable old sum bitch."

The action was entirely out of character for a man who wore a seersucker suit, bow tie, and suspenders. His thinning white hair was topped with a fedora and a fancy hat feather, chosen to carefully color coordinate with the tie. The bow tie was his trademark, and he had an extraordinary collection to select from.

He returned to the kitchen and called Virgil Thompson at the Conoco garage and service station just off Main Street. Virgil was the only mechanic Doc Adams would let touch his Packard. Virgil understood the urgency for getting Doc Adams to the clinic, so he dropped what he was doing and headed over to West Central. With little time to investigate, Virgil finally drove Doc Adams to the clinic in his pickup truck and returned to work on the Packard under less pressure.

Registered Nurse Audrey Ann Daugherty was in a snit. When the doctor didn't arrive at the expected hour, she went into her well-practiced panic mode, making the other two staff members very uncomfortable.

"Well," she said, wringing her hands, "where do you think he's at?"

Missy Siler, bookkeeper, and Wilma Williams, receptionist, looked at each other with raised eyebrows as if somehow they were expected to know.

The first appointment of the morning was a monthly regular, seventy-six-year-old Thelma Lou McKendry, who suffered from a near terminal condition known as aging. She walked with a slight list to starboard, had a nervous twitch in her left eye, talked with a lisp, took a large daily dose of pills, ached all over much of the time and made certain everyone around her knew about it. Thelma Lou suffered in a number of ways, but never in silence. She didn't mind at all if the doc was late, the clinic was exactly where she wanted to be. Thelma settled in and expected special attention from the women present.

"I know he is on the way and will be here any minute," said Nurse Daugherty. "Can we get you anything, a cup of coffee or water?"

"No," smiled Thelma Lou. "I'll be just fine, but I do have this nagging pain in my shoulder. It just won't go away, been killing me all week."

"Could we get you an aspirin, or something stronger?"

"I'll just wait 'til Doc Adams gets here."

Roscoe Simmons came in right after Thelma, checking on the exact time of his early appointment. He was in work boots, overalls and denim shirt, and he smelled of diesel fuel. He had a Cleveland Indians baseball cap sitting slightly askew on his balding head. Wilma Williams knew everyone in Medford and greeted Roscoe as he came through the door.

"Sorry, Roscoe," said Wilma. "Doc Adams is running a few minutes late this morning. Just have a seat over there and he'll be with you as soon as possible."

"Well, what's the holdup?" asked Roscoe.

"He's on his way, just take a seat."

"I got lots of important stuff to do this morning, don't have a bunch of time to be sittin' 'round waiting."

"I'll tell you what, Roscoe," said Wilma, "if what you got to do is all that important, I'll be happy to reschedule your appointment for another time that's more convenient. Then you can jest run along and get to your important stuff."

"Nah . . . I'll wait a few minutes. It really don't make me no never mind." Roscoe smiled to himself, realizing the receptionist had called his bluff, making him sound and look a bit foolish.

Doc Adams came through the door in a rush. "Good morning, folks," he said. "Had a little car trouble this morning."

He took off his jacket and hat, handing them to Missy in exchange for the white medical smock she had in her hands.

Thelma Lou followed him into the examination room without invitation.

"Have a seat, Thelma," he said. "How you feeling today?"

"Truth is, I'm not sleeping well and my stomach has been acting up. Might a been something I ate, but I don't know for sure. I cooked up a right large mess of collard greens night before last and that might a been it."

"Probably not," said the doc.

" I don't know what's the matter with my left knee, seems to ache most all the time. I also have some right bad pains in my shoulder."

"Have a seat up here and let me take a look."

"I swear to goodness, I just don't know what's the matter with me, Doc." Thelma went on without taking a breath, "I don't have a lick of energy these days."

Doc Adams motioned for her to open her mouth and he peered in while holding her tongue down with a wooden depressor. He did this as much to keep her quiet for a moment as to satisfy her need for medical attention. He put his stethoscope to her chest without speaking, listening as he moved it around from spot to spot.

"Tell me about your meals, " he said. "What do you have to eat on a typical day?"

"It's right hard fixin' for just one," she answered. "I know I don't eat regular as I should."

Doc Adams looked at her chart, reviewing the medicines prescribed.

Thelma leaned forward, looking directly in his eyes: "I was also worrying about whether my veins are okay," she said. "I mean do you think they're getting to be close?"

"What do you mean?"

"My sister Louise who lives in Lake Village said her doctor told her she had very close veins, and she's gettin' some kind of treatment for it."

"I believe her doctor meant varicose veins, Thelma. Believe me . . . that's not your problem."

"What's wrong then?"

"Thelma Lou, here's what I am prescribing for you. I want you to go over to the Safford County Grill at lunchtime today and order the Blue Plate Special. Then, I want you to eat and enjoy every single bite of it. The candied yams are especially good. Then, I want you to have a nice breakfast every morning. You also need to try walking at least thirty minutes every day. Promise me you'll do that."

"Well," she said with a frown, "if you think it will help."

"And another thing. I want you to bring in all your medicine bottles the next time you come. Bring in every single one of them. I need to check what you are taking."

Other than car troubles, the day was off to a typical start. A parade of the local infirm trooped through his examination room all day long, several actually in need of medical attention. Doc Adams told the members of his Wednesday night poker group that Safford County suffered from an epidemic of hypochondria. If folks didn't have a serious ailment, they invented one. It seemed to be a part of the culture.

Roscoe Simmons worked at the gas company, delivering tanks of propane or refilling tanks at farms in the outlying area where this was the main source of heating and cooking. The ancient truck he drove all week had a weary diesel engine. Somehow Roscoe managed to spill diesel fuel on his clothing every time he filled the tank, thus the trailing aroma that followed everywhere he went. Roscoe sat on the examination table with his shirt off.

"How's that indigestion? Is the medicine I prescribed doing any good?"

"Nah, Doc. It comes back every night and sometimes it's hard to breathe."

"Roscoe, you need to level with me. Do you take the medicine just as I prescribed it?"

"I try to, Doc, but it ain't always easy."

"Another thing . . . does the indigestion come back before or after those two or three stiff bourbons you have every night?"

"I don't have 'em every night."

"Didn't I tell you that it could damage your liver, if not the lining of your esophagus, and that I couldn't do much for you if you kept it up."

"Doc, I told you I was going to quit drinking at the start of the year."

"Well," Doc Adams said with a sigh, "did you?"

"I did for a fact and I can tell you it was the worse two weeks I've had in quiet a spell."

"Please tell me you meant that as a joke, Roscoe."

Round and round the doctor-patient conversation went and Roscoe left with another promise that he would faithfully take his medicine and cut down on the nightly sour mash.

Medford is a town of small-time merchants, a smattering of professionals and several large landowners who grow soybeans and cotton on acres and acres of the Delta's rich, dark soil. There are many truck farms, selling their goods at a large open market near the town square. In season you can find Bradley and Traveler tomatoes, squash, a variety of peppers, watermelons and new potatoes. Some folks drive from miles around on Saturday mornings to visit the Medford Farmers' Market.

There are the usual establishments: two dry cleaners, one pharmacy, one midsize department store, two banks and several locally owned restaurants. In addition to the Stafford County Grill, the Meet 'n' Eat is perhaps the most popular, featuring good old down-home Southern cooking. There is also a small, private airport just west of town where two operators offer crop dusting services, primarily for the large corporate farms. Medford's young people have to drive the forty-two miles to Lake Village to go to a movie or to pass time at a bowling alley, a circumstance they complain about incessantly.

A parade of patients continued through the clinic during the morning. There were the usual sniffles, one problem with a severe sprained ankle and an emergency case of a suspected broken arm. Theodore Wesley, the seven-year-old son of Coach Alex Wesley, history teacher and coach at Medford High School, had fallen through the monkey bars on the school playground at recess and the duty teacher was certain his arm was broken. This resulted in an emergency stop at the principal's office and a quick trip to Doc Adam's clinic. Teddy's arm was bruised and he had shed a few tears, but Doc Adams assured them all that he would be okay. Back to school he went with his arm in a sling, an all-day sucker, and the admonition to stay off monkey bars for the remainder of the week.

Doc Adams took a coffee break and finally found time to visit the restroom. When he came out Wilma was waiting to give him a set of car keys and a message from Virgil Thomson.

"Virgil said tell you he had to replace the battery and you shouldn't have trouble starting the car in the morning."

"Did he say how much that costs?"

"Just said he'd be sending you a bill . . . and he mentioned that the timing chain didn't sound right."

"What's a timing chain?" asked the doc.

"I don't have a clue," she said. "You know I don't know nothing about engineering."

"Well, how might a faulty timing chain alter engine performance?"

"How would I know," she said with a sigh.

"Well, Wilma, do you think I should be worried about it?"

"The only thing I think," she said with a smile, "is that you need to call Virgil."

Doc Adams loved to pick on Wilma, asking her opinion on a wide variety of things, including local and state government issues, recent medical journal findings, and touchy international affairs. She knew exactly what he was doing . . . certain he knew the subjects were of no interest to her whatsoever. If these items did not appear in the Style Section of the *Arkansas Gazette* or near the daily crossword puzzle, she was not acquainted with them.

As Missy, Wilma, and Audrey were discussing arrangements for lunch, a stranger came in and looked around, carefully inspecting the waiting room. They knew almost everyone in Mayford and did not recognize the man. He was six-feet tall, slightly unkempt, with sandy brown hair in dire need of a barber's attention. His khaki pants were soiled and wrinkled and barely touched the top of a pair of snakeskin cowboy boots.

"What can we do for you?" asked Nurse Audrey.

"I need to see the doctor."

"Did you have an appointment?" asked Wilma as she returned to her station behind the reception desk.

"No, but I was passing by on the highway and need to get some relief from the pain."

Nurse Daugherty stepped forward. "What pain?"

"I have a history of kidney stones."

The women sprang into action, just as they were trained to do, eager to provide medical assistance to any person in distress. They both had experience with kidney stone patients.

Wilma and Missy had the stranger take a seat, got him some water and tried to comfort him as Audrey rushed in to alert Doc Adams to the emergency.

Doc Adams came out of the examination room and introduced himself. "Are you having sever pain right now?" he asked.

"I don't think so, but it's hard to tell. I've had it before and I just need something to help me through it."

Doc Adams ushered the man into his examination room as Wilma followed behind with an armload of the appropriate medical forms.

"We'll have him complete those later, Wilma," the doc said as he waved her back out the door.

"That don't matter," said the stranger. "I always just pay for everything in cash."

The man identified himself as Alex Hampton, from Memphis. His story was that he was a merchant seaman and had to make it to

Mobile, Alabama, the next day to join the crew of a cargo vessel bound for some port in South America. The passage would take more than sixty days, and he told the doc he needed a painkiller prescription for pills that would last him at least for the first month. His drug of choice was Dilaudid.

Doc Adams sent him into a restroom with a small plastic cup and instructions to provide a urine sample. The stranger stepped into the bathroom and was there for a few minutes. He returned at the sound of a toilet flushing and handed over the cup. Doc Adams called Audrey in and instructed her to process the sample.

While waiting Doc Adams asked how long he had been suffering from kidney stones, and how many separate attacks he had experienced. Alex was not clear in his answers, suggesting that he couldn't remember exactly how many and when he experienced it last.

"I've been suffering with a thyroid condition for many years," he told the doc, "and the kidney stone problem has lasted over several months."

Back in the waiting room, Wilma noticed a Ford pickup parked at the end of the clinic's driveway with a man sitting in the driver's side. While she prided herself on knowing everyone in Safford County, she had seen neither the truck nor the man before. It seemed unusual to her that someone would be just sitting in his truck in the clinic parking lot at this hour. The Louisiana license plate caught her eye.

Doc Adams gave Mr. Hampton two tablets and a cup of water, suggesting that he take them immediately. He did so.

The doc went out to check on Audrey's progress. She reported in a breathless whisper that there were traces of blood in the man's urine.

Back in the examination room, Doc Adams probed further as to the nature of his troubles; that is, when the first kidney stone attacks occurred, what treatment was given and where? He examined the man's back and sides, checking for tension and trying to determine the severity of his pain, if any. Doc had treated many sufferers over the years and Alex Hampton's demeanor did not fit the usual pattern. Most of his kidney stone patients arrived in severe pain, desperate for relief and offering no resistance to a hospital bed.

Doc Adams recommended the stranger consider going directly to the emergency room of Stafford Medical. Alex Hampton insisted his condition was not that bad and that he had to move on. He stressed the fact that he had to get to Mobile on time in order not to miss the ship and lose his job.

So, Doc Adams wrote out a prescription for a minimal number of Dilaudid tablets, adding a strong recommendation that the man go to an emergency room for x-rays and treatment to make certain he did not have permanent damage to his kidneys.

Alex Hampton paid the receptionist in cash, made a hasty retreat out the door and left with the man in the pickup truck, the truck with Louisiana license plates.

Claudine McAlester had been preempted by the stranger and was clearly upset that she had to wait longer than anticipated to see the doc.

"Sorry to do that to you, Claudine," said Doc Adams. "Do you know anything about kidney stones?"

"My sister's husband, Freddie Mac Brewster, had an attack last year and he said it was a worse pain than giving birth."

"That's the usual sentiment," said the doc. "A man just came in off the highway saying he was having pain from kidney stones. I felt he needed emergency attention, and I hope you understand."

"Well, yes I do. But I don't know how my brother-in-law could compare kidney stone pain to giving birth since he ain't never give birth to no baby."

"You have a point, Claudine. Now, what can we do for you today?"

Her blood pressure was too high, as was her weight. After a hasty examination and prescription for some medicine for the hypertension, Doc excused himself and hurried back to the front desk, asking Wilma to get Sheriff Baxter on the phone.

Roland Baxter was an ex-marine who served in several military police posts, including a long stint at the main gate to

Arlington Cemetery. He returned to Safford County and joined the Medford Police Force. Three years later he was elected sheriff and was a fixture in the law enforcement circles of Southeast Arkansas.

"Here's Sheriff Baxter," said Wilma, handing him the phone.

"Thanks for taking my call, sheriff," he said. "I just had an unusual situation here that I thought you might want to look into."

"What's that, Doc?"

"A man was in here with a story about kidney stones, insisting that he needed a sixty-day supply of Dilaudid."

"What's a delogged?"

"No, Dilaudid . . . it's a narcotic, actually a hydrogenated form of morphine."

"Why did you give it to him?"

"He said he was suffering from kidney stones, and it's appropriate to treat the pain with a mild narcotic like Dilaudid. With traces of blood in his urine I thought I had to do something. However, I prescribed only two dozen pills, not the sixty-day supply he was looking for."

"What do you suspect?"

"I don't know, but the whole thing seemed out of line. I would suggest you check at the Stafford Pharmacy to see how eager he is to fill the prescription. He had some traces of blood in his urine and his blood pressure was elevated, symptoms that would support such a condition. Still, somehow this didn't seem right. I have treated many kidney stone cases, and this fellow's actions just didn't add up. Most people suffering from kidney stone movement aren't so calm. In fact, they are usually in excruciating pain. I thought you ought to know about it."

"Kay Max Doggett is my brother-in-law," said Sheriff Baxter.

"He's the new pharmacist, right?"

"Correct. I'm on my way over there right now."

"Have him call me if he has any questions."

"What was the man's name?" asked the sheriff.

"Alex Hampton, and he said he was from Memphis. "

"Thanks, Doc, I'll get right on it."

"By the way sheriff, Wilma said he was with another man in a green Ford pickup with Louisiana tags.

"I'm heading for the Stafford Pharmacy right now!"

Doc Adams went back to his practice, seeing a number of patients with similar problems. A flu-like virus was making the rounds in Medford and his appointment book was filled for the week. Marline Banister was next in line, eager to tell the Doc about the pain in her left shoulder.

"When I get up in the morning, it jest aches something fierce," she whined.

"Have you done anything physical to injure that shoulder, Marline, or is it just that old Ritis boy acting up?"

"What Ritis boy?" she asked, clearly confused by his reaction.

"You know Arthur," he grinned. "He always was the worst one of those Ritis boys."

Marline then got the joke, but didn't laugh. Arthritis did not strike her as a funny subject.

Doc Adams continued his examination, all the while thinking about the Memphis man and wondering if he had done the right thing.

Within minutes Sheriff Baxter was at the pharmacy talking with his brother-in-law. Hampton had been there, paid cash for his prescription and left minutes before. Kay Max was surprised by the amount of the prescribed dose of Dilaudid but was hesitant to question Doc Adams. He had only taken over the Stafford Pharmacy six months before and was still uncertain about the medical practices of the area. He didn't want to start his new career at the pharmacy by offending one of only three doctors in the county.

Doc Adams left the clinic at dusk after seeing the last patient, leaving Audrey the task of preparing for the next busy day and closing the clinic. Audrey put in almost as many hours at the job as he did. He treated her like a business partner and made certain she was paid well for her efforts.

Doc Adams closed his eyes and turned the ignition switch, hoping the ancient Packard would start. He smiled as the engine coughed and responded. He still had rounds to make at the hospital before a late dinner at home with Marcia. Through forty-six-years of marriage, Marcia had grown accustomed to his kinetic schedule, accepting the role of companion and supporter, realizing that she simply had to share her husband with a community of country folks who loved him almost as much as she did.

Marcia had spent most of the day in her volunteer role at the new Stafford County Library. In fact, she headed up the fund-raising project that helped create the library. She especially wanted the young people of the county to share her love affair with reading.

Marcia's timing was perfect, born of long experience with her husband's tiring schedule. She had just placed the spaghetti and meatballs on the table when he pulled the Packard into the garage.

"I have garlic bread in the oven," she announced as he took off his hat and coat.

"Thanks a million," he said. "I'm starved."

She poured two fresh cups of coffee as he sat down to eat.

"How was your day?" she asked.

"Marcia, my love," he smiled, "it was the most unusual day I've experienced in a long time."

"How so?"

Unfolding a napkin for his lap, he said, " I might as well start at the beginning!"

He told her about the Packard's battery problem, his tardiness in arriving at the clinic, and worked his way through the highlights of the parade of patients he saw during the day.

"Thelma Lou McKendry was in again this morning," he told her. "That woman is a walking case of hypochondria. She even asked me if I thought her veins might be too close together."

"I feel sorry for her," said Marcia. "She has been so lonely since her Herman died."

Doc Adams put his coffee cup down and pushed back from the table, actions accompanied by a deep sigh. "I have to tell you about the real incident of the day. It involves what I believe to be a fake kidney stone problem and a possible narcotics scam."

"A narcotics scam, what are you talking about!" She moved her chair closer. "Right here in Medford?"

Several months later the following story appeared on the Associated Press wire:

LOUISIANA MAN GUILTY IN PRESCRIPTION PLOT

Little Rock, Ark. – *Alexander R. Hampton convinced six doctors across a three-state area that he suffered from a thyroid condition and painful kidney stones and that he needed larger quantities of a narcotic painkiller. He told the physicians that he was a merchant seaman about to embark on a long trip abroad.*

Hampton was putting on an act to get multiple doses of the drug Dilaudid and had made up the stories, authorities say. Dilaudid is a form of morphine that is usually prescribed as a painkiller for cancer patients.

Hampton, 42, of Shreveport, Louisiana, was convicted in Pulaski County Circuit Court on six counts of obtaining a controlled substance by false representation. He faces up to five years in prison for each count.

David Brookfield, an assistant prosecutor, said Thursday that Hampton's act had been so convincing that he had received more than 1,200 tablets of the drug from area pharmacies with prescriptions he conned from doctors in Louisiana, Arkansas, and Mississippi.

Hampton's attorney, Christopher McWerter, said in his closing argument that Hampton had been addicted to Dilaudid and should not be sent to prison "for what the doctors did to him." McWerter blamed the medical profession for turning Hampton into an addict.

In his closing statement, Brookfield argued that each

doctor Hampton visited had offered him medical assistance and recommended emergency room treatment. Hampton rejected treatment on the fictitious grounds that he was going to the Mediterranean Sea or the Persian Gulf on a freighter.

Brookfield also noted that investigating officers had found a syringe of blood in Hampton's coat after his arrest. He said that Hampton had used the syringe whenever doctors wanted a urine sample to verify a kidney stone condition.

According to police an accomplice of Hampton's was not charged. The drugs were never recovered.

Courthouse Capers

Millersville, Arkansas
Population: 6,408

Buster had just shifted into third gear after gaining enough speed to make it up the rise toward Buck Hill. At that very moment he caught sight of the station wagon pulling out of Elm Street directly into his path. He grabbed the steering wheel with both hands and slammed on the breaks as hard as he could stomp! That was not enough effort.

The log truck was leased to the Davison Lumber Company and was loaded with long leaf pine trunks approximately twenty-four-feet long. The weight was well over the limit approved for that type rig, a standard practice of Davison and the loggers. The truck sagged in back and the shock absorbers strained to keep the frame off the axle. Driver Buster Leroy McDougal was making his second run of the day with a load picked up at a logging site fifteen miles north of Millersville. He was to deliver the timber for processing at Davison Lumber, the largest employer in town.

Trappers and riverboat people established Millersville, a sleepy town located in the southeast corner of Arkansas, in 1825. It remained a small community of farmers, merchants and loggers.

Lillian Adair was heading south on Elm Street in her 1954 Ford station wagon. She had just picked up dry cleaning from the North Side Laundry. She was trying to decide how to deal with an ailing mother in Dermott, another Arkansas Delta community just down the Mississippi River from Millersville. Her mother could no longer take care of herself at the family home and had reached the stage where professional nursing care would be required.

Lillian agonized over the prospect of dealing with the burglar in her mother's life. The thief was an early onset of Alzheimer's, gradually stealing her personality, then her memory. Lillian was struggling with the nursing home realization, daydreaming her way down Elm at the speed limit. Her mind was on a new assisted living facility as she turned the corner from Elm to Main.

With wheels locked and breaks squealing, the log truck slid into station wagon, catching it broadside on the passenger's side, crushing that door and driving the vehicle halfway down the block before it came to rest. Dust and smoke rose from the hood of the station wagon. Buster jumped from the running board of his log truck and dashed around to see if the driver was hurt.

Lillian's right hand and arm tangled with the steering wheel and she was knocked hard against the driver's side door. The collision scared her to death but she was not seriously injured. Two cars stopped to investigate and offer assistance. Someone across the street called the police dispatcher and a city patrol car arrived within minutes. Buster insisted that Lillian be taken to Mill County Memorial for a checkup and to make certain she was not badly injured.

The city patrolman made a routine written report, noting that the driver of the station wagon had pulled out onto Main Street without observing a stop sign. The log truck suffered minimal damage and no charges were filed.

The following week a short news item and photo about the accident appeared on the front page of the *Millersville Record.* That's what prompted the telephone call from a law firm in Little Rock.

Lillian's husband Marvin ran the service station at the corner of Main and Wexford streets. His big Texaco sign dominated that side of the town square. This was not a modern service station. Marvin managed the business by himself, employing two teenage boys for the weekends. He still came out to pump gas, wipe windshields and chat with all the customers, many of whom he had seen the weekend before at the Bethany Baptist Church.

The lawyer got Marvin's phone number and called before the week was out. He was very solicitous of Lillian's condition and eager to learn all he could about the details of the accident. Marvin told him all he knew, explained that Lillian was not seriously injured, and thanked him for his interest.

Attorney Raymond W. Martin, of the firm of Brooks, Henry, Martin, insisted on driving down from Little Rock to determine the extent of damages and the potential for a substantial lawsuit against the lumber company. He had a clerk check records to get an idea of the size of the lumber company's admitted assets. A big old insensitive lumber company taking advantage of a poor lady driver was just the kind of action his firm specialized in.

The Mill County Courthouse was in the center of the town square, built by the proud citizenry in 1921. The courtroom, located on the second floor, was typical of dozens in small courthouses all across the south. It was constructed of dark oak paneling and had a dank smell of mildew. Judge Franklin W. Parnell presided.

Judge Parnell looked the part. He was just over six-feet tall, slightly under weight, had white hair that formed a half circle rim around his head from ear to ear. He also had bushy white eyebrows. Judge Parnell spoke in a slow, drawn out Southern accent. He had presided over every major court case in the county since anyone could remember.

The subsequent lawsuit filed against the town's largest employer, the Davison Lumber Company, was driven entirely by the work of the big city lawyer from Little Rock. Marvin and Lillian expressed concern from the start about how their neighbors and the lumber company management would react. After all, Marvin had to do business on the town square and Lillian had dozens of special friends there. However, Attorney Ray Martin was very persuasive, assuring them that they deserved substantial compensation from the big old uncaring lumber company.

Realizing the potential of the company's deep pockets, and fairly certain of an out-of-court settlement, he had insisted that Lillian file charges. While the log truck had hit Lillian's station wagon broadside at the intersection of Elm and Main, everyone in Millersville knew the story; that is, that Lillian ignored the stop sign and was clearly at fault.

The arrival of the well-dressed attorney from Little Rock and the action against Davison was the sole topic of conversation for days on end at Doggett's Confectionery, Harriet's Hair Care and at Casey's Barbershop. While Lillian's car was damaged opposite the driver's side, it could be repaired. The citizens discussed the facts in exhausting detail.

Doug Rockford, owner of Rockford's Hardware, and Willard Brannon, editor of the *Millersville Record*, actually got into a heated argument about the subject over morning coffee at Doggett's Confectionery the following Wednesday.

"We have been dodging those overloaded log trucks for months," said Willard. "It's about time Davison had its comeuppance."

"Well, we can always count on the liberal press to ignore the facts and the law," countered Doug. "Does it matter to you at all that Lillian was at fault? Did your reporter miss the fact that Lillian ran a stop sign and pulled out in front of the truck?"

"I believe that's for the court to decide. . . . I mean, whether she was at fault or the log truck driver. At the *Record* we will just reports the facts in the news story, but you can count on my opinion on the editorial page."

"Well, that don't matter cause nobody reads your editorial page anyway. You'd be better off putting your opinions on the sports page or in the obituaries. That's all anyone ever reads."

"You're wrong again, Doug. I get good feedback from our readers all the time about our editorials."

"Complaints mostly?"

"A few."

"Well, Willard, my good man, the truth is that the *Record* is the only newspaper I know of that you can pitch in the air and read before it hits the ground!"

"Now you're getting insulting, so I'm going to work."

The court proceedings got underway three months later. Judge Parnell, rather distinguished-looking in his black judicial robe, seemed uncomfortable from the start. The courtroom was packed with itinerate legal experts, some actually taking vacation leave from Davison to be there. They wanted to see how this lawyer, who had taken the largest suite at the Mill County Hotel on the square, and who appeared always in a very expensive suit and silk tie, would show up these southeast Arkansas hayseeds.

Attorney Ray Martin made his opening statement, strutting up and down in front of the jury. It was obvious to all present that he held himself in very high esteem.

"Ladies and gentlemen of the jury," he spoke in a measured, deliberate tone, "it is important for the citizens of this county to know that regular, everyday people such as Lillian Adair must be protected from the remarkable hubris displayed by large corporations. People should be able to drive the streets of this city without the expectation that a large, multiton log truck, driven by an inconsiderate driver, would crash into the side of your automobile with the possibility of extreme bodily harm."

Several of the jurors looked at each other with raised eyebrows. Osborn Sangster, custodian at the Millersville Elementary School, asked Mavis Tucker sitting beside him just what the word hubris meant? She shook her head, indicating she didn't know.

He called to the witness stand an elderly black man who lived in a rundown frame house on Elm Street, just across the street from the accident site.

"Will you swear to tell the truth, the whole truth and nothing but the truth, so help you God?" asked the bailiff.

"Yes, sur, I will," he answered, adding as an afterthought. Everyone knows I don't lie none anyway."

Striking an authoritative pose before the jury, Ray Martin began to present his case. "Please give this jury your full name."

"Well, sur, my name is George Lewis Jones."

"And, Mr. Jones, your birthday is August 30th, is that correct?"

"Yes, sur, it is."

"What year?" he asked.

After a thoughtful pause, George Lewis said, "Every year."

The members of the jury ducked their heads in muffled giggles and tried not to look at each other. Judge Parnell held a folder of papers up to his face in an effort to maintain some aura of judicial decorum.

"I mean just how old are you?" asked the attorney, realizing that his superior standing before the court had been slightly bruised.

"I jest had my seventy-eighth birthday," said George Lewis.

"I see that your address is listed as 203 Elm Street. Is that correct?"

"Yes, sur, it is, that's where me and the missus live."

"On the morning of April 12 of this year . . . "

"Me and the missus . . ." George Lewis wasn't finished. "Been liv'n in that same house nigh on to forty years."

"Well, good," said the attorney, "but on the morning of April 12 of this year you were sitting on your front porch of that same house just about a block from the intersection where the accident occurred. Is that correct?"

"Yes, sur, I was."

"And you witnessed the accident?"

"Yes, sur, I seen it."

"What were you doing on the front porch at that time of the morning, Mr. Jones? Maybe having a cup of coffee, or reading the morning newspaper?"

"No, sur, I wasn't reading no newspaper cause I didn't have my eyeglasses."

Attorney Martin raised his eyebrows and took a deep breath. He paused for special effect. In an effort to create more anticipation he turned his back to George Lewis, raised his chin high and took several steps toward the jury. With increased volume and a measured voice for dramatic emphasis he asked, "Mr. Jones, just how far can you see without your eyeglasses?"

With a second to think, and in an effort to be helpful, James Lewis said, "Well, sur, I can see de moon. . . . How fer is that?"

The courtroom exploded in laughter. The jury doubled over and slapped each other on the back with uncontrolled joy. Judge Parnell abandoned any pretense of decorum and laughed out loud.

The big city attorney from Little Rock shrugged his shoulders. For a moment it appeared he would make the effort to gather himself, reestablish his lofty standing in the courtroom, and return to the attack. He paused, took a deep breath, changed his mind and slumped back toward his desk.

"No more questions of this witness."

The trial lasted through noon the next day with the jury unanimously ruling in favor of Davison Lumber Company. Lillian and Marvin Adair didn't seem at all disappointed. They were actually relieved, as were the judge and citizens of Millersville. George Lewis Jones found himself in a new position of celebrity for the rest of that summer.

Raymond W. Martin, attorney at law, returned to Little Rock having learned a valuable but costly lesson; that is, there are many things about a small Southern courtroom not covered in law school.

No Forwarding Address

Savannah, Georgia
Population: 132,000

He poured a second cup of coffee and opened the *Savannah Morning News* to the Coastal Empire section. He scanned the page and was amused to find that many of the facts in his obituary were in error. They can't get anything right he thought to himself.

At least the name was correct—Evan W. Hughes.

The duffel bag at his feet carried the initials RWH. His new name would be Robert W. Houston, one he had worked hard to create months before as he made arrangements for a new life. He had searched through all the cemeteries in and around Savannah, Georgia, looking for a tombstone with exactly the right information. Finally, on the North side of Bonaventure Cemetery he found a grave with the name Robert W. Houston, a boy born in 1963. The grave marker contained the notation that "The Houston family's beloved Bobby died at age four of a childhood disease." Evan knew that Bobby had not lived long enough to establish much of a legal identity, including Social Security, driver's license, credit cards or a passport. Using the family name, and a well-crafted letter, he was amazed at how easy it was to obtain a copy of the boy's birth certificate. From there it was no problem obtaining a bogus driver's license, Social Security and credit cards.

His thoughts raced about this crazy scheme, so unlike anything anyone would expect from a buttoned-up insurance tax specialist. This was a major turning point in his life. He was just fed up with what his world had become, ashamed of his own behavior of the past several years and disgusted with himself for the foolish error in judgment. This was to be a fresh start, the future he might have created had it not been for that one big mistake.

Margaret O'Brien was that one big mistake. All her friends at Georgia Southern University knew her as Maggie. He got reacquainted with her at a college reunion three years before. He knew her from the several dates they had during his senior year, none of which were especially memorable. She had blue eyes, a terrific figure and a casual mane of ash-blond hair. At thirty-three she still turned men's heads, and knew it. Both were then lonely and rebounding from failed five-year marriages, neither of which had produced children. He graduated from Georgia Southern, located in nearby Statesboro, Georgia, in 1983, earning a bachelor's degree in business. She was an art history major, interested in no particular career, concentrating primarily on partying and shopping.

The salt air of the morning had a nice feel to it as he opened the window and looked out at the beach. The south end of Tybee Island was a bit shabby, packed with storefront businesses and fast food restaurants. There were the usual pizza places and T-shirt shops. This was his filth and final morning at the Raven Motel. He was eager to go, knowing that he must keep a very low profile until the news, as he wanted to see it, was confirmed. He had been biding his time, living on diet sodas, pizzas and sandwiches, watching for the ending of a special news story. It first appeared on the front page of the *Savannah Morning News*, then as a follow-up piece for the next three days in the Coastal Empire section. Finally, it appeared as an obituary at the week's end. That was his signal to continue executing the master plan. Steps one, two and three had gone rather well he thought.

After a short courtship and quick justice-of-the-peace marriage, Evan and Maggie returned to Savannah, where he worked as a tax insurance specialist with a well-established brokerage firm located just off Wright Square. He had earned advanced financial planning designations, was NASD licensed, and took on the more complex business insurance cases for the firm, especially those where there would be tax consequences.

When they were settled in a downtown apartment, Maggie applied for several jobs, or so she told Evan. She reported that nothing ever seemed to work out. She always had a good reason why she wasn't selected for the job. She seemed content as a lady of leisure. He tried with discretion to help her find employment, but finally realized the well rehearsed litany of excuses meant she had no intention of working. That was somewhat different than the impression she gave him before they were married.

Tybee is a Georgia seaside resort town eighteen miles east of Savannah. The main attraction is a three-mile long beach, backed by sand dunes covered in sea oats, and a pier and pavilion with families and friends strolling the boardwalk at all hours. Evan selected the area as his initial stop because of its proximity to Savannah, access to the Bull River, and because it was considerably less hectic at this time of year. He chose the Raven Motel for the same reason, assuming he could stay there a full week in anonymity if necessary. When he checked in, slightly damp and disheveled, the elderly woman behind the front desk didn't bother to look him in the eye. She took his credit card and checked him in, trying desperately not to miss a moment of the television program she was watching. That was just what he expected, and just what he wanted.

His troubles with the new wife began within months after the marriage and their homemaking efforts in Savannah. At first they enjoyed late evening strolls in the historic district and had several favorite restaurants within walking distance of the apartment. The sex was also good at first. Their conversation and companionship was simply okay, but any attempt on his part to discuss issues of the day or future plans and objectives was met with a vague indifference. He tried to introduce her to some of his friends, tried to suggest outings with other couples he thought she might enjoy, but she quickly developed a small cadre of girl friends that consumed her interest and time. She and the new friends made frequent shopping trips to Atlanta, Charleston, Hilton Head, and Jacksonville. Her tastes in clothes, shoes and jewelry were at the high end, as their MasterCard statements clearly demonstrated.

He began to check the credit card purchases regularly and became concerned about the ever-increasing debt. When he approached her to discuss excessive spending she launched a neurotic pouting act, dismissing his concerns with a disconcerting air. Since he was a successful insurance broker, making lots of money, she wondered why he should worry if his wife occasionally bought a few nice clothes and pieces of jewelry.

Then there was the unexpected trip to New York with two friends from a gated community on Skidaway Island just southeast of town, a golf and boating community called The Landings. She simply announced on a Thursday morning that they would be leaving early the next day for a long Manhattan weekend of shopping and Broadway shows. She didn't discuss the trip with him in advance, didn't ask if he minded, and didn't invite him to be a part of it. She also ignored any attempts on his part to find out more about their plans. He could feel the resentment grow in his gut, and he began to seriously question what this relationship held in store for the long term. He was confident that she was not interested in another man. Her efforts seemed directed entirely toward impressing her girlfriends and working her way into a larger social circle.

On those weekends when she was preoccupied with travels or shopping, he retreated to his boat, spending long hours on Wassaw Sound or exploring the many rivers and creeks off the Intracoastal Waterway. He enjoyed being alone on the water, fishing for whiting and sea bass, or just experiencing the extraordinary wildlife. He could cruise into any number of pristine creeks or rivers and drop anchor. His twenty-three-foot Cobia had a cuddy cabin and a 225 horsepower Yamaha engine, enough size and fuel capacity to travel almost anywhere in the region. He had named the boat for his first wife, *Happy Hannah.*

Just before he and Maggie were to be married, he changed the name of the boat and made the appropriate registration adjustments for state regulators. He did this in spite of the old adage that it is bad luck to change the name of a boat. This time he named her the *Pretty Penny*. Before their marriage, Maggie expressed interest in his boat and fishing, and told him how much she looked forward to overnight trips with him on the Intracoastal Waterway. Shortly after they were married, she let him know that she really didn't care that much about boats or the water, feigning a tendency toward seasickness.

The last straw with Maggie—actually the last two straws—arrived in the form of the final bill from the New York trip and her new insistence that they move out of the apartment in the city and build a new home at The Landings. She had racked up a $5,870 New York weekend with her friends. As to her interest in building a new house, she had actually toured Skidaway Island with one of her travel buddies, picked out a lot on the marsh that she simply could not live without, and made an appointment with a real estate agent for them both to tour the property and to discuss a purchase price. All this she had also done without consulting him.

His instincts ran to a new level of frustration, then genuine anger. He used a client meeting as a handy excuse for postponing The Landings real estate appointment, and immediately began to form a plan to deal with her increasingly intolerable behavior. He was fed up with her and furious with himself. After all this time he didn't really know the woman. She lived in an alternate world of her own design, oblivious to the real one. He blamed himself. How could he have been so foolish as to marry her on such short notice and with so little foresight or forethought? That was so unlike him. He was the analytical one, the person who had to think things through and organize plans, the person his fraternity brothers relied on to take charge of major activities. He had suffered through the agony and expense of one divorce already. It had been the low point in his life and he vowed never to experience that again.

By sheer coincidence, the client he had to meet that weekend was Ralph Blackwell, owner of a chain of appliance stores with outlets in Savannah, Hilton Head, and Bluffton. Ralph was also a Georgia Southern graduate and had married a friend of Evan's first wife, Hannah.

Ralph had done well in taking over his father's business, expanding the number of stores, producing a consistent operating gain. He insisted on a Saturday breakfast meeting with Evan to accommodate his weekday work schedule. Ralph needed help and advice in establishing a 401(k) financial plan for his growing number of employees. In addition, he had questions about the business insurance required to back up a loan needed for the purchase of inventory. Evan explained what steps were necessary for both and offered several options for Ralph to consider. They agreed to meet again the following weekend after Ralph had talked things over with his store managers.

That accomplished, they ordered another round of coffee and began reminiscing about college days. Ralph casually asked Evan how his new wife was doing. The question was posed in a way that blended courtesy with curiosity.

"It's none of my business," said Ralph, "and I shouldn't be telling you this, but Maggie's first husband, Michael Law, and I were fraternity brothers."

"Really," said Evan. "She rarely has anything to say about him, except that he was abusive and she simply had to leave him."

"Well," squirmed Ralph, "I've heard the other side of the story in detail. According to Michael, she was spending him into bankruptcy, constantly traveling on her own without him and running up bills that were unbelievable."

"Tell me more."

"Mike described her as a freeloader who had no sense of what it took to earn a living, and who seemed interested only in his bank account and how she could spend it."

Evan tried to act nonchalant, indifferent, but it was evident he was intensely interested in what Ralph had to say.

"I shouldn't be telling you this about your own wife, and I apologize for even bringing the subject up. Sorry . . . I'm very sorry, I was clearly out of line."

"No, don't be," said Evan. "I know you were just passing along information and I actually appreciate your telling me this. Why don't we just let it go at that?"

In spite of what he now considered a monumental mistake, Evan was a very thoughtful and methodical man. He made plans for how to accomplish things. He made lists of "things to do." One by one he got them done. That's how he approached his brokerage business and why he was very successful in representing a full portfolio of well-to-do clients, mostly successful small business owners. He had devoted the last decade of his life to this business and it was becoming uninteresting and routine. The compensation was good, but the subject was tedious and constantly changing. Congress continued to tinker with the tax code each year, requiring a new learning cycle for professionals in the financial services industry as well as the expense of retooling software systems and the necessary forms. He had been considering a change for some time, even thought about law school. Maybe this would be the time. Boredom with the job and frustration with a marriage led to his organized approached to a new master plan. There would be several major steps. He wrote them on a yellow legal pad at his desk:

Step One: Begin the quiet rearrangement of assets; move several amounts in small increments over time; use multiple financial vehicles; create layers of transactions to generate distance and a difficult-to-follow paper trail.

Step Two: Study how to reinvent yourself, to establish a new identity. Begin the process of obtaining bogus new driver's license, credit cards, Social Security number, and more.

Step Three: Purchase a cheap used car and stash it in a nondescript lot on Tybee Island; scout out an appropriate landing area; find a quite, low-end motel close to the landing area, and a large Dumpster nearby for disposing of equipment no longer needed.

Step Four: Study the tide charts and prevailing winds to determine the most appropriate date and time for execution of the plan's major move. Do a test run to scout for unexpected circumstances or obstacles.

Step Five: Study business climate of Miami, Florida, and the

Bahamas, check out most ideal living areas and determine a timetable for seeking employment.

Step. Six: Execute plan on time and date selected.

Over a period of several weeks, Evan had moved the things he needed to his boat which was stored in a rack at the Savannah Bend marina. No one at the marina paid any attention to his trips to the boat while in the first-floor rack. A sign posted just inside the storage area cautioned boat owners about entering boats while in a rack. He knew this was for insurance purposes, covering the Marina in case of a lawsuit resulting from injury climbing in and out of boats.

Evan pulled himself into the boat by a ladder at the transom, entering through the fish door. He did this with ease, as did many other boaters at Savannah Bend. At dusk one evening he delivered a small, inflatable life raft and two paddles. On another evening he brought a light electric trolling motor and battery. He found the raft one Saturday while strolling through Keller's Flea Market south of Savannah. The one-person rubber raft was still in its original box and had never been used. A bargain, he thought, at $40. He followed up another item in the classified section of the *Savannah Morning News*. Someone on Ogeechee Road was trying to sell a well-used Minn Kota Classic twenty-eight pound trolling motor. At $38 the motor was a bargain, and he could find a 12-volt battery anywhere. He would need to jury-rig a system for attaching the motor to the raft, but he had time to tinker with it.

Evan had constructed his own tide chart, tracking the phases of the moon to determine the best day, and night, to make his move. He was looking for a high spring tide, resulting from the moon's closer proximity to the earth. The tides along the coastline around Savannah ran an average of six to nine feet. The extra few feet provided by a spring tide would produce a slightly faster flow of incoming current, making it easier for him to complete his plan.

Finally the day was chosen when the moon and earth aligned as needed. Evan had read about an art exhibit on St. Simons Island, scheduled for that same weekend. He asked Maggie if she had plans to go.

She did not, but he had planted the idea, and she took the bait. Maggie called a few friends to see if they would like to make it a day trip. They, of course, looked for any reason to spend the day on St. Simons Island. Evan knew they couldn't resist dinner at one of the several nice restaurants there and would not return to Savannah until very late in the evening.

When that special weekend finally arrived, Evan drove to the Savannah Bend Marina and had *Pretty Penny* lifted out of its rack and into the water. He bought frozen squid and live shrimp for bait, asking several questions of the crew about what others were catching and where. He filled his tank at the fueling dock and shoved off down the Wilmington River past the old Palmer Johnson Marine Services facility and out toward Wassaw Sound.

From the Savannah Bend Marina it would be about fourteen miles to the Atlantic, traveling directly out the Wilmington River, past Skidaway and Wassaw islands. Skidaway, home of The Landings community, is one link in Georgia's Pleistocene barrier island chain, an eight by three-mile stretch of land that would have been oceanfront property at some stage during the last Ice Age. This is where Maggie was pressuring him to move, insisting they build a new home, another attempt on her part to improve her social standing and open doors to a wider circle of friends and activity. Evan found no logic in such a move, and was certain she was clueless as to what it would cost to build a home in the island community.

A salt marsh, tidal creeks and several small hammocks separate Skidaway and Wassaw islands. Wassaw, an uninhabited exterior barrier island, is a wildlife refuge that may only be visited during the day. Evan enjoyed cruising around Wassaw, fishing occasionally for red drum, flounder and sheepshead along the seven miles of undeveloped beach. He found extraordinary peace on the waters near the island, home of migratory fowl, including numerous species of shore birds, the endangered wood stork and several bald eagle nests. The beach also provides a nesting habitat for loggerhead sea turtles, and is the home of piping plovers and peregrine falcons. A spit of sand juts out at the north end of Wassaw, and rolling swells increase in the sound with winds from the north and east. On more than one occasion, Evan found that moving his boat up to anchor close to the beach could be tricky business. Cruising around Skidaway and Wassaw and exploring the many miles of tidal waterways around Savannah would be one of the things he would miss most in a new life.

The ruins of an 1898 Spanish-American War fort are visible at the northeastern end of Wassaw, and that's where Evan began to make a swing to the north, far enough out in the sound to pick up deeper water. He would steer the *Pretty Penny* toward Little Tybee Island and the deeper water channel at the mouth of the Bull River. He was familiar with these waters, having fished often at a favorite spot near Green Channel Marker "3." That's where he stopped and dropped anchor.

He put out two fishing rods, rigged for bottom fishing. He would spend several hours pretending to fish, thinking about his new plan, and trying to imagine what the rest of his life would be like. An occasional sports fisherman motored up or down the river, but for the most part the afternoon was quiet. High tide would peak at 11:45 P.M., with the incoming current strong enough from 9:30 P.M. on. He needed the current coming in to help him reach his destination in the raft. He caught and released an occasional whiting or small bonnet head shark. He ate two ham sandwiches, finished a small bag of potato chips and drank several diet sodas during the long afternoon. As the sun moved down behind Wassaw Island, he began preparations for the launch. Few fishermen or recreational boaters are on the water after dark. The ability to navigate, to see channel markers and to estimate distances becomes more difficult and movement seems more exaggerated at night. Boat traffic along the Bull River ended at dusk and the moon appeared as a signal. It was time.

Evan started the engine in neutral, pulled up the anchor, went back to the helm and eased the boat back into the Bull River. He maneuvered the craft near Little Tybee beach where he sailed a wet Tilley hat with his name and telephone number stenciled inside. He moved the *Pretty Penny* farther up the Bull River, far enough from the sound to make the raft trip shorter but not so far that the boat would not drift back out as far as possible into Wassaw Sound. He again stopped the boat, dropped anchor and began preparations. He used a foot pedal air pump to inflate the raft. A small wooden board had been fashioned to fit at the back of the raft, providing a platform of sorts for attaching the electric motor. The arrangement, while not entirely satisfactory, was stable enough to hold the motor. He dropped the foot pedal pump into the water and watched it sink. Next, he eased the raft over into the river on the starboard side, tying it to a cleat at the transom. He carefully placed his duffle bag, a 12-volt battery and the two paddles in the rubber craft. He checked to make certain his knife, flashlight and hand-made chart were still in his jacket pockets before bringing up the anchor.

The Cobia was already drifting across the Bull River toward Little Tybee Island as he untied the raft and started paddling. The going was tougher than he had imagined and the tidal current was not as accommodating as he had hoped. He was now in a one-man raft in a wide river with thirty feet of water under him. He attached the cables to the battery terminals and turned the electric motor switch. The propeller labored to move the raft, producing a steady thrust with the current. The electric motor was designed for lakes or still waters and was put to a new test in a tidal river such as the Bull. Paddle he must, and paddle he did. After a time he looked back to see the blue bimini top in the early moonlight and the *Pretty Penny* drifting in the middle of the river. Then he laughed out loud at the irony of his sudden thought. He had changed the boat's name when he remarried, but forgot to change the beneficiary designation in his $500,000 life insurance policy. It still listed Hannah (Moore) Hughes as the primary beneficiary. That should result in some interesting legal tussles, he thought.

It took a full hour to reach the mouth of Lazaretto Creek. The electric motor labored on as he paddled, and his arms and shoulders began to ache. He must maneuver his raft to make his way to Tybee Creek. The tide would be of little assistance once he made the turn, and there would be another three miles to Tybee Island. He simply had to stop and rest his arms and back. The raft drifted to the south bank of the creek near Morgan's Cut. He was near some craggy cedar trees and ragged palms, most of their crowns having blown off. The small wooded area seemed to rise out of the surrounding tidal waters. Prickly pear cactus and bush palmetto carpeted the surface on the far side of the hammock, the only land he could see. The waterscape looked very different at night, and the trip he had made numerous times was not so familiar in moonlight. He had to refer again to the homemade chart. He tied the raft to an overhanging limb and stretched out as best he could to rest his head on the side. Positioning himself in the raft to rest was awkward at best. The moon was his major source of light and the water glistened before him.

Evan was startled by the sound of an outboard motor getting louder and louder, another sizable boat coming toward him from Tybee Island. If he were sighted, those in the boat would surely stop to investigate. The law of the sea dictates that all boaters are responsible for each other, and respond to the rescue of any boat or person disabled or in distress. Why would one man in a small rubber raft be out in the edge of Tybee Creek at this hour of the night? Any boat captain would automatically assume the person was in trouble. Evan squeezed down as flat as possible in the bottom of the raft, trying his best to make no movement at all. The motor craft sped by at some twenty knots and the driver did not see the raft. The boat, however, threw a large wake as it passed and Evan was rocked to the point of thinking the raft would turn over. It remained upright but did take on a significant amount of water, something Evan was not prepared for. He frantically scooped water up with his hands and dumped it over the side of the raft, more quick work for arms that were already spent.

Across the marsh to the north Evan could see an eerie set of lights moving slowly from left to right across the horizon. The silence of the night, the moonlight casting shadows at the water's edge and the view of a long row of lights made the whole scene surreal. He wasn't sure for a moment that all this was actually happening. None of his family or childhood friends would ever believe Evan W. Hughes would make this kind of decision, putting himself in this awkward position. He had second thoughts about the wisdom of this move. A nervous feeling came over him, a marginal panic of sorts. Maybe he should consider turning back, maybe the *Pretty Penny* hadn't drifted too far. What was he thinking? His arms and back would never get him back to the sound in that little raft. He took a deep breath and looked again at the moving lights, realizing now that they were from a huge container ship on the Savannah River, heading out from the Port Wentworth Terminal toward the sea buoy and beyond.

The night would not wait so Evan shoved off and moved back into the creek. Without that trolling motor, he thought, he could never have made it this far. Even so, the battery was getting weaker and a new whining sound foretold the certain demise of bearings in the motor. The going was slow and his arms were becoming numb. After another thirty minutes he gave up on the motor and battery, realizing they were only adding weight to the raft and not helping him now. He loosened the motor from the board, tossing it over the side. The battery followed closely behind without a splash. He would just have to paddle the rest of the way.

After what seemed like an eternity, lights from the beach town appeared before him. This gave new life to his effort and the raft moved deliberately and silently toward the spot along the shore that he had identified weeks before. He heard music and loud voices from somewhere nearby. He hadn't expected anybody to still be partying at that hour, but the party was on. His target was a stretch of muddy beach near AJ's Restaurant on the south side of Tybee Island. The lights at the dock were on but the restaurant was closed and dark.

Evan changed plans at the last minute, deciding to stop at the far end of AJ's dock. There he would leave the creek and dispose of the raft and paddles. He cut a gash in the side of the rubber raft and there was an instant *swoosh* of air. He slung the duffle bag over his shoulder and tried to scoop the raft into a manageable armful. In so doing he soaked his shirt and the front of his pants.

Three days before he had stashed an old beat-up car in a nearby driveway of a small beach house for sale. The house had seen much better days and the lawn was overgrown with weeds. The house was in serious need of renovation and a drainage problem was evident at the street. A Realtor's FOR SALE sign included an out-of-town telephone number. Evan left the car parked in the driveway with a FOR SALE sign in the window. He changed the Realtor's last telephone number from a nine to an eight with a marking pen. He then put the same number on his auto sign. He walked several blocks to a large hotel near the beach and took a cab back to downtown Savannah. The gamble was that the auto would remain there for at least three days.

It was approaching midnight as he walked around the corner to the vacant house and his car. The 1989 Chevy Cavalier was still there, covered with dust, a very tired auto he had purchased the week before from a man in Pooler, Georgia. It was offered in a small newspaper used car classified section. Evan paid cash for it and gave the fellow a false name and address. The seller grinned as he took the money and asked no questions. In a few days, maybe a week, he would use this car to drive out to Interstate 95 and head south. The plan was to have lunch in Jacksonville on that day, abandon the Chevy for a newer used car, purchase some respectable clothes and spend the night in another motel on the other side of Jacksonville.

Maggie returned to Savannah later than expected. The girls wanted to have dinner at a favorite restaurant in St. Simons. She noticed that Evan's car was not in its usual parking spot and was surprised that he was not home. Maybe he had a late meeting with a client. He typically told her about such late appointments in advance. She remembered that he had planned a fishing trip out to Wassaw Sound. She called the police around 1:00 A.M. to report that her husband was missing. The dispatcher had questions and she answered as best she could. Yes, he had planned to go fishing. Yes, he was in his own boat. No, she didn't know the name of the boat. No, she couldn't remember exactly what kind of boat it was or what size. No, she didn't know exactly where he usually fished. Yes, he kept the boat at the Savannah Bend Marina.

The Coast Guard was notified and a search began. The early morning hours produced patrol boats and a helicopter, using information provided by the crew at Savannah Bend marina. They provided the name and description of the boat, captain's name and attire as he left, and potential areas for his fishing trip. Evan's car was still in the Savannah Bend parking lot. The Coast Guard quickly found the *Pretty Penny* aground in a shallow area called Wassaw Breaker just off the Bull River channel. Then the search began for Evan W. Hughes, white male, age thirty-four, six-feet tall, sandy hair and blue eyes, last seen aboard his twenty-three-foot walk-a-round boat heading out Wilmington River toward Wassaw Sound.

A small article appeared on the front page of the *Savannah Morning News* the next day, reporting on the lost fisherman and the search under way by the police marine patrol and the U. S. Coast Guard. A Coast Guard helicopter from the air station at Hunter Army Air Field spent several hours searching the creeks, hammocks and helping coordinate the efforts of search vessels. After forty-eight hours with no findings, and no appearance on any of the surrounding islands, the Coast Guard changed the classification from a search to a recovery mission. His Tilley hat was discovered by picnickers on Little Tybee beach but there was no body, no Evan W. Hughes.

The following morning's article moved to the Costal Empire section of the paper and offered little hope of finding the missing fisherman. Cold, hard statistics about people lost at sea, quoted by a Coast Guard spokesman appeared as a well-rehearsed masterpiece of accommodation; that is, carefully avoiding declaring the person lost and neglecting the use of any words of encouragement.

Two of Maggie's close girlfriends stayed with her, tried to comfort her, and tried to offer hope that Evan would magically appear. Maggie was distraught, but her concerns seemed a bit strange to her friends. She was upset about her potential status as a widow; concerned about the loss of income, financial security and the thought that she might have to go back to work. She expressed disappointment about the fact that there would likely be no new home at The

Landings. And, incidentally, she was also concerned about losing her husband of two years.

The president of Evan's brokerage firm called every day to check on Maggie, offering assistance in any way she needed it. They were very pleased with Evan's work, saw him as a rising star in the organization, and struggled with questions about how to handle his book of business in the interim.

Conditioned by the unusual spring tide that weekend, the Coast Guard made an assumption that Evan had fallen overboard and was carried out to the sound by a strong tidal current. A swimmer on Tybee Beach had been swept out to sea and lost the month before. Evan's fishing gear was still in place, tackle box open on the deck, live shrimp in the bait well, and the fish door open at the transom. Everything in the boat suggested the captain had left unexpectedly. Coast Guard officials thought the fisherman had somehow fallen overboard but would not make such a public statement for news purposes. In similar cases, bodies did not show up for days, if at all.

Evan gathered his things and packed his duffel bag. He checked out of the Raven Motel and headed for the west side of Savannah, Interstate 95 south, and on to a new life. He was amused by the thought that there would be no forwarding address. He planned to lose Evan W. Hughes and reemerge in South Florida as Robert W. "Bob" Houston. He would need to get used to the new name, repeating it out loud to himself: "Bob Houston . . . Robert W. Houston . . . Robert Wilson Houston."

Things went well in Jacksonville. He found another cheap motel on the south side of town and the next morning set about getting a haircut, shopping for a new casual clothes, and looking for a suitable used car bargain. He traded the Chevy for a late model Ford pickup.

He pitched his meager belongings in the truck, pulled out into Interstate 95 traffic, turning south toward Miami. His chest was filled with a strange tension, a combination of fear and excitement. But somehow it felt good!

A Willcross Farewell

Willcross, Arkansas
Population: 2,643

It was her first holiday trip back to Arkansas after a fifteen-year absence. Not her first trip, but the first Thanksgiving. This was actually her second return home since graduating from high school. Six years before she had returned to help Granny Tyler celebrate her eightieth birthday. This time was different. The memories came back in volumes, some much too painful to think about and a few remarkably soothing. The personal demons still existed for her in this tiny corner of the world.

The direct TWA flight from Dallas landed in Memphis shortly after noon. She bought a sandwich and soda in the airport, rented a Hertz midsize and headed across the Mississippi River Bridge into Arkansas. She turned south just past West Memphis and headed toward the Delta. The scenery seemed strangely unfamiliar. In the past this flat land was the center of her universe and the small town of Willcross her only reference point to reality. From a new and wider perspective it was almost as if she had never been there before.

The landscape hadn't really changed that much: lonely silos, muddy backwater, a long, tapering horizon and fields now lying fallow. A scattering of sharecropper shacks still stood parallel to the highway, located just beyond the railroad tracks. Flocks of crows lined the high wires and guarded the irrigation ditches below. Maybe it was she who had changed.

Rebecca Ann Covington was returning this last time for only one reason: to attend the funeral of her grandmother, Eula Mae Tyler.

Granny Tyler was the matriarch of the clan, the human adhesive that held together what little family was left. Becca's father and mother never really understood or accepted their role as parents, leaving the job of raising a son and daughter to Granny Tyler. Granny was far better equipped to handle the task anyway. One aunt and uncle remained in Willcross, stubbornly clinging to a way of life that the young people of Willcross were abandoning. Aunt Francis and Uncle Otis Covington lived two blocks over from Granny Tyler and had been keeping a close watch on her welfare. Otis had been general manager at the Willcross Cotton Gin, retiring at age fifty-five when the operation closed. This traditional crop of the Delta had gradually given way to soybeans and the cotton gin had to change to a part-time operation, no longer able to make a regular payroll.

The exodus began soon after Willcross youngsters quit school or graduated. They made a quick and permanent exits in search of larger opportunities and experiences, to places such as New Orleans, Little Rock, Memphis, and points west. Becca's academic record in high school—valedictorian of her graduating class—helped win a generous scholarship to Delta State, located across the big river in nearby Cleveland, Mississippi. That represented her only chance to attend college, and she knew it. In a compact three years she earned a degree in English and international marketing, compiling a grade-point average that attracted recruiters from a number of corporations, especially a large advertising agency in Dallas. She took the job and advanced quickly within the company, earning a national reputation in the process. The pay was impressive and her bonuses extraordinary by Willcross standards. She now earned at least three times the average income of anyone back home.

Becca drove past the street to her grandmother's house and continued on to the cemetery behind the Willcross Methodist Church. She wanted some time to herself. As a troubled teenager, she had often come to this cemetery to think, and to have a good cry when she needed it. This visit to her old haunt was an attempt to minimize the time she might have to spend with any family members who had already arrived, and with whom she had little in common. She dreaded having to make small talk with the elderly friends and neighbors who, would no doubt, be gathered in the kitchen of her grandmother's modest frame house on West Elm Street.

Becca specialized in pharmaceutical product campaigns and success begat success. She designed and presented marketing programs—including detailed plans for product positioning, point-of-sale literature, billboards, print and media advertising—always followed by public opinion research to determine effectiveness. Her marketing plans were new to the industry and inventive. The positions she created for the products were always provocative, but not controversial. These were well-constructed campaigns that the manufacturers eagerly implemented, and she was in demand at industry conferences to discuss advertising strategy and tactics. She brought positive publicity and new clients to the firm, and was well-compensated for her efforts.

Just as in high school and college studies, Becca found refuge from her emotional discomfort by focusing exclusively on the work. This was her defense mechanism for avoiding the painful feelings of emptiness associated with growing up in a dysfunctional family and the resulting inability to trust others in personal relationships. She had no close friends in Dallas, only business associates. She did not let men get close to her emotionally. She had very few dates over the years, always businesslike and all having to do with official industry events or local charitable organizations. She carefully avoided any intimacy with the several men who expressed interest in her, making it obvious to them that she was devoted only and entirely to her career and work.

Becca didn't know if her younger brother Ray would return to Willcross for the funeral. They were not close. In fact, she hadn't heard from him in over five years, not since his divorce from high school sweetheart Peggy Louise Franks. Peggy was the daughter of a neighbor couple, close family friends of their parents. At least, they used to be friends. Raymond Wade Covington married Peggy right out of high school, electing to go to work for the Delta Southern Railroad as a brakeman.

He didn't "care nothing about no college degree," he told Becca. Besides, he announced to the family with some bravado, that he was now "making good money." The railroad hours were irregular and the travel schedule didn't accommodate a new and fragile marriage. As it turned out the "good money" wasn't good enough. The divorce was ugly and the breakup included both families. The Covingtons and Franks also parted company.

Becca Ann had been sending Christmas cards to Ray at his last known address in Biloxi, Mississippi. They were never acknowledged and she didn't receive anything in return. Last time she called his telephone had been disconnected with no explanation from the official prerecorded message.

The Willcross city limit sign was turned sideways, hanging at an angle as she drove pass. The sign announced a population of 2,643. That was about the same number of local citizens she remembered from fifteen years ago. The village consisted of a long row of stores on the east side of the main highway with the railroad tracks on the other. The courthouse square was one block over from the main highway, surrounded by a scattering of storefronts, including a pharmacy, hardware, clothing store, used furniture place, Merchant's & Planter's Bank, real estate agency and the only decent restaurant in town, Hogan's Cafeteria.

Willcross High School buildings were not what she remembered. Grades seven through twelve had been eliminated and the few students left in those age groups were bused to a consolidated school in nearby West Helena. The former high school had been converted to an elementary school, educating the dwindling number of children in grades one through six. A small, stand-alone gymnasium with parking lots on one side stood out against the playground in back. Becca Ann had played two years on the junior girls basketball team and remembered the little cracker-box gym as a dark and smelly place. Her teams never produced a winning record.

She noted that almost half the stores along the highway side of town were now boarded up. The Willcross Drug Store had plywood over the windows and a big CLOSED spray-painted on the glass door. This was where she and several other girls had spent long Saturday afternoons thumbing through movie magazines and ordering a succession of cherry Cokes or strawberry milk shakes.

Several pickup trucks were parked on a side street. The owners were no doubt engaged in the major activity of the day, snooker played in the back of The Crawfish, a combination café and pool hall. The front half of the building contained a sandwich shop with pool and snooker tables in the rear. Several pinball machines lined the wall in between. At the far end of the strip was a rundown Texaco Station, the only other business alive at this hour of the afternoon.

She parked the rental Oldsmobile between the church and cemetery, noticing the change of colors in the trees: burnt orange, tangerine, bright reds and yellows. The change of seasons had no such impact in Dallas. Towering oak trees lined the back of the cemetery fence and there was the fresh clean scent of new-cut grass. The contrast to her life in the city was dramatically apparent: miles of concrete and tall buildings versus towering trees, the smell of grass and open space. More inner conflict. The seasons and atmosphere took on a new importance. Becca missed the former and needed the latter.

She opened the iron gate to the cemetery and closed it behind her. The latch clicked as she stepped inside, noticing a newly dug grave site to her left. It was located at the edge of the area where aunts, uncles and her father were buried. This was surely being prepared as Granny Tyler's final resting place. Becca felt a growing lump in her throat and fought back tears. This was the one loss she was not prepared for.

Oh yes, her parents! While she had grown up in the same house with Elizabeth Ann and Thomas Covington, they had always seemed more like distant relatives than parents. Her mother didn't like to clean house, didn't do laundry and was a marginal cook. She spent much of her days reading pulp novels, sneaking out at night after supper. She drove around the back roads by herself in the family pickup truck and smoked an endless supply of Camel cigarettes. The tobacco left a yellow residue on her fingers and a lingering stale, sour smell on her breath. Her mother's evening odysseys did not include alcohol. She didn't even like the taste of liquor or how it made her feel. Small comfort: while her mother had not been a drunk, she clearly was dealing with other personal demons.

Her father was a tall man, probably six feet, with thin gray hair. He was skinny and had unusually long fingers. He always wore a white dress shirt with no tie, and a vest that displayed a pocket watch and chain. Thomas Covington also seemed ill at ease around his wife, unable to make even light conversation. Their marriage was a strange one.

One morning Thomas discovered that his wife's single cardboard suitcase was missing. She had disappeared with it. He found out a week later that she had run away with a drummer from New Orleans, a real sporty-type fellow in a new Ford station wagon, who came through town selling farm implements and a revolutionary type fertilizer. No one had a clue as to where they went. Thomas didn't seem at all upset by his loss, and made no effort to find his wife or to inquire as to her whereabouts. In fact, in some ways he even seemed relieved by the whole of it.

"That's just the way life goes," he was overheard telling the boys at the hardware. "You win some, lose some, and some gits rained out!"

Ray and Becca were left to fend for themselves, unless Granny Tyler was present. Their father was a clerk at the one hardware store in Willcross and only worked when he felt like it. The owner didn't mind his itinerate schedule because business was slow and he only really needed Thomas when he had to be away for any reason. Thomas knew the hardware business and could help customers with advice about almost any type home project. In that sense, he was especially handy.

Ray spent most of his time at home with his father, while Becca depended more on her grandmother. How they all made it through the school years was a mystery, but Becca closed out all the sorrow a girl goes through without a mother's guidance by losing herself in her schoolbooks. She studied with a passion and was determined not to accept less that the top grade in every class. As a result, she was an excellent student, well thought of by all her teachers.

After Becca's mother skipped out on the family, her father treated her as an inconvenience. He frankly had no idea about haw to raise a teenage daughter. Her needs and wants were simply a puzzle to him. At least he could talk sports and hunting with his son.

Her brother cared little about studies and busied himself with hunting, fishing, and borderline illegal activities with his buddies. He was also a regular at Peggy Frank's house, a fact that was not entirely acceptable to her parents. They were all pleased and surprised that Ray was able to graduate from high school.

It was unusually quiet at the cemetery, especially compared to police, ambulance and fire sirens in Dallas. Becca stopped at the site of the new grave and looked down at the plastic cover over the opening. Granny Tyler had been the only link she had to family lineage, the only person she trusted with her deepest fears and loftiest dreams. Her grandmother was the only one in the world who ever really knew her, who offered advice without strings attached. Becca wasn't certain she understood the whole concept of love, but if she loved anyone at all at any level, it was her Granny Tyler. And she thought Granny Tyler was the only person who actually loved her. Becca never knew her grandfather. Douglas Edward Tyler—known by the family as Pop Pop—died in a hunting accident before she was born. So, her father had grown up without a man in the home.

Becca knew she was expected at about this hour at the old house on West Elm, but something made her want to stay longer at the cemetery. She walked to a nearby flat headstone and sat, watching as a red tail hawk soared overhead. The winged creature circled for a second time, settling on the highest limb atop one of the live oaks. A breeze moved in to cool the late afternoon air, sending a slight chill down her spine. Becca's thoughts returned to her last visit with Granny Tyler, the day after her eightieth birthday party. She had arrived the day before and, at her grandmother's request, stayed an extra day after the guests had gone. They both longed for some private time together.

The next morning after the birthday celebration, Granny Tyler began the eighth decade of her life by making a large pitcher of sweet tea. She and Becca sat at the kitchen table and talked, a return to the same kind of conversations they relished when she was an awkward and confused teenager, experiencing all the problems associated with those difficult years, problems compounded by the absence of a mother and the presence of a detached father. It would have been so easy to use this as an excuse to give up, to drop out, and to leave for a larger city and another life. Granny Tyler was the reason she did not.

"Lord'a mercy, sugar, I am so glad you came home for a visit," she said. "I have missed seeing you so very much."

"I wouldn't have missed your party for anything, Granny, and I have needed you far more that you could know."

Her grandmother was showing the effects of aging. Becca had not seen her in this condition. Her eyesight was bad and she could not hear well. This was also the first time Becca had seen her walking with a cane, and she moved about with considerable difficulty.

"You don't need me any longer, sugar," she said. "I brag about you all the time at church and the library . . .those are about the only places I get to nowaways."

Becca spoke louder to make certain her grandmother could hear. "I have been promoted to vice president of the agency now," she said. "I don't believe I told you about that."

"You have done very, very well, sugar," she smiled. "You look so professional and you dress like a real lady. Truth is, you've grown up to be a very special person."

"Granny, you make me blush."

Becca tried to act casual about the compliment, but it was exactly what she wanted and needed to hear, especially from her grandmother.

"I've just worked hard and have you to thank more than anyone for pointing me in the right direction. In fact, I received a nice raise this year and have been earning some very good bonuses. If you need any financial help of any kind at all, Granny, I can . . ."

"No, no, sugar, you keep that money and do something for yourself with it." After a pause to catch her breath, she added, "What I really need is something your money can't buy!"

"What's that?"

"My energy and good health back. I don't know if it's the years or just the mileage, sugar, but something is catching up with me."

Becca had been suppressing a lingering uncertainty for years, an insecurity conditioned by the difficult childhood and the absence of a give-and-take relationship with parents. Of all the emotional forces that influence personal behaviors, insecurity has the most insidious power. This emotion wore many disguises for Becca, especially during her teenage years.

Her grandmother was the wisest and most stable person she had ever known, with a depth of understanding and a storehouse of information greater than even the professionals she worked with in her industry. Her grandmother amazed her. With her academic and business success, Becca was still dependent on the acceptance and support of Granny Tyler, a support she provided simply by being alive.

Becca's grandmother did not have a formal education, but she volunteered as head of a small county library established in a former utility building on the courthouse lawn. She kept the library open on Mondays, Wednesdays and Fridays from 1:00 to 5:00 P.M. She didn't have that many visitors, so most of her time there was spent reading.

Her unusual wisdom came from native intelligence, a practical common sense, and her voracious appetite for reading. Since her husband's death, she had taken over the little library. The task was not too demanding and it gave her the opportunity to read through a steady supply of books, primarily nonfiction works in history, psychology, business, and public affairs. She also loved biographies, searching always for threads of interests or patterns of behavior that ran through the lives of successful people.

In these long talks during her formative years, Granny Tyler recognized the convincing disguises Becca used to mask her uncertainty and that helped her overcome the sense of loss she felt about her mother and unstable home life. Granny Tyler had read much about the socialization of a child, understanding that a sense of being loved is what makes a youngster want to learn good habits and behave with respect and courtesy. She made it her cause to replace Becca's fear with extra affection, making certain she knew she was valued, that she had opportunities for much more in life. Granny Tyler gave her the tools for self-appraisal that led to maturity unlike that of anyone else in her immediate family.

Becca felt both gratitude and guilt about the special attention she received and for the advantage it provided. Why did she feel so much better, so much smarter and capable, than her brother and father?

Granny Tyler also tried to provide help for Ray, but he didn't respond. He wasn't even congenial with his grandmother, avoiding any serious discussions other than asking for spending money. Ray seemed strangely detached from reality, with his insecurity leading him in another direction. He managed to deal with it in less constructive ways. Becca finally gave up trying to talk with her brother about anything of substance.

Granny Tyler lived on Social Security and a modest interest income from a savings account. Her home was paid for and she had few needs other than medicines for high blood pressure and the arthritis that plagued her knees. In spite of this, she carried herself with a stature and dignity closely observed by Becca.

Granny Tyler had an ancient tablecloth that at one time had been white; at least, much whiter than at present. She also had eight cloth napkins to match. They had been a wedding gift from her parents, an extravagance they could ill afford at the time. It was a gift intended to demonstrate a great affection for their daughter. The items carried special meaning for Granny Tyler. They had been washed hundreds of times, hung on the clothesline to dry, carefully ironed and put away each week. Every Sunday, for as long as Becca could remember, Granny Tyler set the dining room table with her tablecloth and carefully folded napkins for each place setting. She gathered wildflowers for the table. This ritual established a state of civility for her little home that she would never abandon no matter what the circumstance. She prepared a brunch for the family every Sunday without fail, usually including fried chicken, mashed potatoes and green beans. She always invited Becca's father and brother to join them, as well as Aunt Francis and Uncle Otis. Too often only Becca and her grandmother were there for the meal. No matter the number, her effort was never abridged nor the decorum compromised.

An old station wagon pulled up and parked at the far end of the cemetery. The maroon paint was faded and substantial dents covered the rear of the vehicle. The luggage rack on top held three ladders, all lashed in place with cords of some kind. The back of the wagon was filled with paint cans and tarps.

A man got out holding a large bouquet of flowers, balancing them in his left hand while trying to close the car door with the other. He looked over at Becca, nodded a greeting and entered the cemetery. She watched as he headed directly to a particular grave.

The man, about her age, wore white painter's overalls and a baseball cap turned backwards. He kneeled at a grave and placed the flowers in a concrete container at the base of the headstone. He stayed in place for some time and appeared to be in prayer.

Becca felt awkward, watching what was obviously intended as a personal and private moment. She turned to walk back to the gate when the man stood and turned toward her.

"Excuse me," he called out "Aren't you Rebecca Covington?"

She looked back at him, surprised by the question. She didn't recognize him at first and was uncomfortable meeting a strange man in a lonely cemetery.

"Yes," she answered. "Am I supposed to know you?"

He walked toward her, appearing older than her initial appraisal. He limped along slowly, favoring his left side.

"I know you don't remember me, but we graduated in the same class at Willcross High."

"Joe Fred Wilson!" she exclaimed. "I didn't recognize you in the painter's outfit."

"I know. That's what I do for a living, if you can call it a living. There ain't that many painting jobs around here nowadays."

"It has been a very long time, Joe Fred. I remember you sitting behind me in algebra class. Seems we both had troubles with algebra."

"I barely passed," he said. "Just what are you doing back home?"

"My grandmother died and I am here for the funeral tomorrow."

"Oh yes, Miss Eula Mae . . . sorry to hear." He lowered his head and sighed. "My wife died seven months ago. I put fresh flowers here on her grave every week."

"I am so sorry to hear that," she answered. "It must be very hard for you."

"I met her in Virginia while I was in the Navy, stationed at Norfolk. I put in eighteen years in fact. I got out on disability."

"Are you okay, Joe Fred?"

"I developed some kind of eye problem, had two operations that didn't help much." He pointed to tinted glasses. "I can still drive around here in the daytime and paint a little."

"How long have you been back in Willcross?"

Joe Fred sat down on a stone across from Becca. He took his hat off, revealing a thin and receding hairline. He appeared weary and in need of someone to talk to. They reminisced about the better days at Willcross and friends from their high school years. He was curious about where she lived, her job, and what life was like in a city like Dallas. She enjoyed the relaxed conversation and lost sight of the time, finally realizing that she had stayed too long and needed to rush on to her grandmother's house.

"I'm running late," she said. "I enjoyed visiting with you but I must go now."

She turned and headed for the gate, looking back to wave good-bye.

"I was friends with your brother in high school," called out Joe Fred, almost as an apology.

She stopped and turned back. "You knew Ray?"

"We ran in the same crowd for a while, but that ain't something I'm too proud of."

"I'm embarrassed to tell you, but I haven't seen or heard from my brother in over five years. I don't even know where he lives."

"That's because he just got out of Raiford a few weeks ago."

"What's Raiford?"

"It's the Florida State Prison."

Becca didn't know what to say. She was obviously shaken by the news.

Joe Fred stepped again toward her with his hands deep in his pockets. "I seen him yesterday at the service station getting gas."

"You saw him here in Willcross?"

"I didn't talk to him but for a minute, and he didn't have that much to say."

They talked a brief time more, speculating about what crime Ray had been convicted of. Joe Fred didn't know for sure, indicating only that he had stopped associating with the group because he thought they were headed for trouble. That's why he left Willcross and joined the Navy.

They parted company and Becca drove to her grandmother's house with a head full of new information and conflicting thoughts. She couldn't decide how to deal with her brother if he showed up for the funeral, or even if she wanted to. She was already battling emotions about the loss of her grandmother, the abnormal isolation from personal family relationships and now a convicted felon for a brother. In times like these she always went to her grandmother for advice, but now Granny Tyler was gone.

There were several cars in the driveway and on the street at the West Elm address.

She carried her bag to the door, opened the screen and was greeted with big hugs and kisses from Aunt Francis and Uncle Otis. They had expected her earlier and were worried that something had gone wrong. Otis took her bag to the back bedroom and Francis began introducing her to the neighbors and friends who had gathered, some in the living room and other spilling into the kitchen.

This was in reality her only home. Granny Tyler had made it so. A real home, she thought at the moment, is a place where you are always welcome for Sunday brunch and good conversation. That was the small frame house on West Elm.

She talked with many of those present, hearing their kind and glowing words about her grandmother. Otis introduced her to the minister, the Reverend Blake Widener, Granny Tyler's pastor for years at the First Baptist Church. The reverend was only part time, having retired years before. The dwindling population of Willcross and the loss of congregation made it impossible to support a full-time minister. The reverend just filled in on most Sundays and accommodated longtime members for marriages and funerals.

He and Becca retreated to a quiet corner of the front bedroom to talk. He knew she had been her grandmother's favorite and wanted her thoughts about the funeral. They talked for a time, reviewing the order of the service and plans for music. As the reverend rose to leave, he asked Becca if she would please be the one to offer a eulogy to her grandmother. This took her by surprise, but she couldn't say "no."

Becca had written and delivered dozens of product promotion presentation for important clients, people who had financial interests tied up in the strength of her ideas and the quality of her proposals. Somehow, this was different. She would do it . . . and she would do it well for the grandmother who had done so much for her.

She returned to the living room to find her brother talking to Uncle Otis. There was an awkward greeting, and acknowledgment of each other's presence . . .without hugs, without kisses, not even a handshake.

Ray was dressed in new blue jeans, a denim shirt and heavy black shoes that looked cheap, obviously government issue. He had stubble of beard, representing several days without shaving. He still had the cocky air, the smarty attitude.

"Where have you been for the past five years?" she asked.

"I been around," was the curt reply.

"I sent birthday cards and notes to the address I had for you in Biloxi, but you never replied."

"I left there some time ago."

"Are you still working for the railroad?"

"Naw . . . I didn't do that but a couple of years."

Uncle Otis joined in to help ease the tension between the two, changing the subject to the funeral and plans for the following morning.

Ray asked what the plans were for Granny Tyler's house, and what would be done with any money she had.

Becca could feel the heat rise in her neck and cheeks, and she fought to control an instant anger. Her immediate thought: he only came back to Willcross for any benefit he might get from Granny Tyler's estate. She wanted to launch a diatribe against her brother, letting all in the room know he had just gotten out of prison, questioning what crime had put him there, and reminding him of just how bad he had treated Granny Tyler when she was alive. Why was he entitled to anything, and why should anyone now consider the interest of a convict?

"Uncle Otis will be taking care of Granny Tyler's estate," she said. "That's not anything you need to concern yourself with."

"I believe I'm due half of everything," he said with a smirk, an obvious comeback to her statement. "You and me are the only family left."

Uncle Otis stepped in quickly to diffuse the circumstance. "This is not the time to deal with any of that . . . our job now is to conduct a fitting funeral service and burial for this great lady. You both will do that with grace and dignity."

Becca turned on her heels, retreated to the back bedroom in search of a pen and paper. She would begin work on the eulogy right now. She changed into pajamas and sat down to think. The words came easy. The light stayed on over the little bedside table late into the night.

The sky was overcast the following morning. There was the scent of rain in the air. Otis stayed the night at Granny Tyler's while Francis returned to their home. No one knew where Ray went, or where he spent the night.

Francis had returned early and prepared bacon and eggs for breakfast. Becca didn't feel hungry, but made an effort not to offend her aunt. By mid-morning, when they left for the church in Otis' Buick station wagon, the sun had made a brief appearance and the sky turned lavender blue.

The Willcross First Baptist Church was already full of town folk when they arrived and extra metal chairs had been placed in the back to accommodate the bereaved. Colorful displays of flowers were at either side of an open wood casket. Reverend Widener opened with prayer and one of Granny Tyler's closest friends, Betty Loraine Udall, played the piano. The pastor spoke of Eula Mae Tyler's role in the community, the large family of special friends she had acquired over a lifetime, and of her passion for reading and learning. He was careful to leave the most poignant memories to Rebecca Ann and the eulogy to follow.

Becca sat in the first pew with Otis and Francis. She scanned the church several time in search of her brother. She spotted Joe Fred Wilson near the back but apparently Ray elected to skip the service.

Becca was introduced, walked to the podium dressed in stylish pumps and a conservative gray dress. There was an eerie silence in the church. Time stood still as Becca begin to speak:

"She called me 'sugar.' I took it as a term of endearment. I believe I was the only one in the family she called 'sugar.' Eula Mae Tyler lived her whole life right here in Willcross. She loved this community, and especially your little library on the courthouse square. This community is so much better off because she lived here. Those of us who were lucky enough to have known her . . . are so much better off for having her in our lives.

"I can't find the words to explain how much I loved . . .or how much I owe. . . this very special lady. She literally saved my life and gave me something to hope far. We sat together many late afternoons at the Formica-topped table in her kitchen, where she filled me with gallons of sweet tea and a treasure of invaluable advice. She told me to always think with my head . . . and dream with my heart.

"My grandmother was a homemaker, born before we discovered feminism and the feminine mystique. She considered being a homemaker an honorable profession, a job where a loving heart was the primary requirement. In that regard, our Granny Tyler was overqualified."

Becca told the congregation about the white tablecloth and the ritual of Sunday brunch at her house. She spoke of the dignity of her grandmother's life and the guidance she gave those smart enough to listen. She praised her appetite for learning and told of the reading habit that lasted a lifetime. She closed her eulogy:

"Granny Tyler was not a child of privilege. In spite of the hardships of her youth, the early loss of her husband, and a lifetime of limited financial resources, I never once heard her complain about misfortune or use those circumstances as a reason to feel sorry for herself or as an excuse for not trying to do her best.

"She was, and will forever be, clearly the most important person in my life. I received from her the guidance of a mother I did not have, the understanding acceptance by a friend I needed as a confused teenager, a level of encouragement and support that was not possessive and which demanded nothing more than love in return."

After the brief graveside service, the family returned to the West Elm house and gathered around the kitchen table. Ray did not make an appearance. Becca told Otis and Francis that the treasured memories of her grandmother would be legacy enough for her. She didn't need income from her grandmother's holdings or anything from the disposition of the home place. Since her uncle and aunt had looked after Granny Tyler all these years, she insisted they take the house and furnishing, as well as any life insurance or other assets left. She would sign any agreement necessary to accomplish a transfer of ownership. If they wanted to include her brother in any way, that would be their decision. She intended to have nothing more to do with Ray for the rest of her life.

Many people asked her for a copy of the eulogy after the service, urging her to make them available through her uncle and aunt. She promised to polish it in some form when she returned to Dallas and to send copies to Otis. Becca went to bed that night with a strange new feeling of relief and satisfaction. The nagging, trailing sense of angst that had plagued her since childhood simply faded away. The thoughts she had about her grandmother and the way she expressed them in the eulogy caused her to reevaluate her own life. The process was liberating. For the first time in many years, she accepted herself as okay, not flawed or inadequate in any way.

She came to the realization that for years she had internalized the childhood uncertainty, the perceived sense of threat, and that she had been preoccupied with self-defense, relying entirely on the long ago feeling of acceptance provided only by her grandmother. Becca was now certain she could manage all that on her own, that a new level of self-confidence was up to her. She no longer had to maintain an emotional residence in "a place apart." Starting tomorrow, she vowed, people would get to know the real Rebecca Ann Covington.

Becca spent the early morning in a round of good-byes to her aunt and uncle and to several close neighbors who came by to wish her well. Her bags packed and loaded in the Oldsmobile, Becca drove north out of Willcross. She turned west on a country road just beyond the railroad station house, following directions provided by Otis. Within a few miles of dirt road she recognized the farmhouse she was looking for. It was set back from the highway with large pin oak trees in front and a picket fence around the front. Joe Fred Wilson's maroon station wagon was parked under one of the trees.

She entered the gate, walked up the steps and knocked. The sound of approaching footsteps revealed that slight limp and Joe Fred appeared at the door, still in his white overalls and denim shirt.

"I came by to thank you for coming to my grandmother's funeral and for talking with me at the cemetery."

"That's nice of you to say Rebecca Ann, but the whole town just wanted to say good-bye to Miss Eula Mae in the proper way."

"I believe we did just that," she said.

Joe Fred invited her in for coffee but she declined.

"I'm on my way back to Memphis and I have to catch a plane to Dallas this afternoon. Before I go I wanted to ask for your help."

"Well, sure." He looked puzzled.

She handed him a white envelope. "When you put flowers on you wife's grave each week, will you please also put a bouquet on my grandmother's grave?"

"I'd be honored," he answered.

"There's enough money in that envelope to cover flowers for at least six months, and a little extra for your troubles."

"Won't be no trouble at all," he said.

"I will send you more when I get back to Dallas."

Joe Fred was pleased to accommodate her, and they briefly discussed the process. She gave him her card and asked that he contact her if he needed more money for flowers or if for any reason he no longer wanted to provide the service. She then surprised herself by doing something that would have been completely out of character for her the day before: she gave Joe Fred a big hug and kiss on the cheek, thanking him again for the favor. Becca Ann left Willcross, heading back to Texas and to a new liberated, demon-free life. This would be her final Willcross farewell.

Two years later the following item appeared in a gossip column in the *Houston Chronicle:*

> *Rebecca Ann Covington, president and CEO of the hottest new advertising agency in Houston, will soon marry Robert J. English, editor and publisher of the highly popular Texas Business Journal. They plan to tie the knot in Bermuda in June and honeymoon in the South of France. Covington Associates, Inc. was cited in the November issue of Advertising Age as one of the top ten new agencies in the U.S. The new couple will make their home in the exclusive Vandemere section of our fair city.*

Epilogue

There is a certain cadence to the language of the South, not to be confused with a drawl. Dialogue has a flavor all its own, especially in the late 1940s and early '50s. This is not the rhythm of language I found in my college studies, such as a class in contemporary American and English poetry. It is not a concern of textbook editors, of math or engineering in particular. Don't look for an entertaining cadence in the style of government brochures explaining the benefits of Medicare and Medicaid. There is a distinctive pace, flow, or singular staccato associated with everyday conversations among the working people of Dixie. I believe I have an ear for that language.

In the 1950s, the fun part of hunting with my father, uncle and grandfather at the Hopewell Deer Camp in Bradley County, Arkansas, was listening to the men exchange banter around a large wood fire at the camp house. I didn't really care much about killing deer, but I loved that time just before daylight, watching the men pour coffee from a large pot resting above the open flames, and listening to their choice of words when regaling each other with tales of past hunts and expected upcoming adventures. The intramural kidding that went on among them every morning was priceless. These were grown men who genuinely cared about each other, relished each other's company, and showed it through the shared an accepted practice of affectionate insults.

"Leroy, you still using that ol' 12-gauge bolt action? You can't hit the inside of a barn with that thang."

The speech pattern was also familiar at family gatherings over holidays or at annual reunions. I listened to aunts and uncles, cousins and kin, savoring the rhythm of the language and the inventive way they expressed themselves. It was not a hurried pace and they just naturally avoided any straightforward explanations.

"Did you see how much weight that Freddie Joe has put on? I tell you . . . that boy can get on the outside of lots of groceries."

The entertainment in the stands was for me equal to that on the field as we attended weekend semipro baseball games at Legion Field in Warren, Arkansas. Loyal fans gathered to cheer on the local boys and offer gratuitous coaching tips from the stands, scolding or encouraging players after each inning. These came in loud voices with errors in the infield or after a close play at first base.

"Get the lead out, grandma. You was running too long in one place!"

Figurative language becomes a natural when you hear it day to day from family, neighbors, friends and coworkers. There is no normal order of construction, and metaphor and simile are used to add strength and freshness to any conversation. There was, in fact, a proclivity for hyperbole. Most of the analogies are invented on the spot, appearing magically out of nowhere.

"I tell you they wern't no moon at all last night, and it was darker than the inside of a cow."

While substance is always more important than style, patterns of speech used to be distinguishable from the Florida Panhandle to the Missouri boot heel. In times past a Southern drawl changed slightly from the Mississippi Delta to the Arkansas Piney Woods, and from the Louisiana Swamps to the rolling hills of Alabama. The emergence of national television produced a standard Midwestern speech, a new familiarity of language that over time has gradually modified speech patterns in the states of the former Confederacy.

I still like to try and hear a difference. If I squint my ears, I can separate a manufactured Southern accent from a genuine drawl. Transplanted, synthetic Southerners are oh so obvious, both in affected speech and adapted culture. A dead giveaway is when an ex-Yankee imposter actually has the audacity to serve guests instant grits. If you want to try the detective work yourself, listen for the absence of an "r" after a vowel, or watch to see if a "y'all" is unconsciously dropped in the conversation now and again.

—Larry Larance

Acknowledgments

Special thanks to the members of The Landings Writers' Club for their tolerance, encouragement and support of my projects. Especially to Barbara Goldsmith who invited me into the group when I landed on Skidaway Island. To Beth—my bride of forty-four years—the Florida State University graduate with a special ear for languages, fluent in both Spanish and French. She encourages my writing efforts, helps with the editing, brags on me to her bridge buddies, and makes certain my subjects and verbs are in agreement. She is a wonderful wife, a terrific mother, an extraordinary grandmother and the best line editor I know. The woman can find an upside down period.

About the Author

Charles Larry Larance was born in Ruston, Louisiana, and grew up in Warren, Arkansas. He earned a Liberal Arts degree at Louisiana Tech University, and holds a Master of Science in Public Relations from American University. As a U.S. Coast Guard officer stationed in Miami, Florida, he served as a flag lieutenant and public information officer during the Cuban Missile Crisis. He spent thirty-five years in the financial services business, retiring as division vice president for a *Fortune 500* company.

Larance has contributed to *Skidaway Musings* and is also the author of *Miss Myrtle's Boy* and *We Count Trees.*

He and his wife, Beth, have one son, one daughter, and five grandsons. They make their home on Skidaway, one of the Georgia barrier islands near Savannah.

Printed in the United States
75220LV00002B/160-354

9 780966 766530